THE MORE YOU SNOW

Alaska Cozy Mystery #16

WENDY MEADOWS

MAJESTIC OWL PUBLISHING LLC

Majestic Owl Publishing LLC
P.O. Box 997
Newport, NH 03773

1

After surviving a pregnancy game show in L.A. that ended up being filled with deadly killers, Sarah didn't mind one little bit that a powerful snowstorm was slowly moving toward the small town of Snow Falls, Alaska, threatening to bury the town in snow and shut down everything. Sarah had come to love the snow—even adore the white winter flakes. The snow had become a close friend that transformed Sarah's world into a white wonderland and kept the real world at bay.

Of course, not everyone in Snow Falls felt as Sarah did, including a little man by the name of Manford, who was fussing up a storm in Sarah's kitchen. "More snow…more shoveling…more ice…might as well be a snowman," Manford griped, sitting at the kitchen table in Sarah's warm cabin eating a bowl of cereal.

Sarah touched her pregnant belly. "Winter arrived early this year," she told Manford, grateful to be dressed in warm charcoal gray sweats and standing inside a safe kitchen. "We're getting a lot of snow."

"Tell me about it," Manford continued to gripe as he gobbled down his cereal.

Sarah smiled. Manford looked handsome in the green shirt and tan slacks he was wearing. His clothes were official "O'Mally's Department Store Employee Attire" that Old Man O'Mally had decided to make all of his employees start wearing. And because Manford had been hired on as an "Official Greeter," the little guy was required to wear the proper uniform, which he hated. "You better hurry or you'll be late for work."

"Work?" Manford asked Sarah and rolled his eyes. "All I do is stand at the front door freezing my tush off saying hey to a bunch of bored shoppers." Manford shook his head. "Let's face it, Sarah, I was hired because Old Man O'Mally feels sorry for me."

"Well...at least he likes you." Sarah struggled to soothe Manford's pride. "Old Man O'Mally doesn't like many people. Besides, you're the one who quit the circus and decided to live in Snow Falls full time and—"

"I know, I know." Manford sighed and raised his right hand up into the air. "I needed a job."

"I offered you a job at the coffee shop."

Manford gave Sarah an *are you kidding me* look. "Sarah, when is the last time you opened up that place?"

Sarah winced. "It's been a few weeks."

"Two months," Manford clarified, holding up two fingers. He shook his head. "I'd go hungry working for you."

"You don't need to work. We have plenty of money and—"

"Hold it right there," Manford demanded and offered Sarah a tired smile. "I know you mean well, and... thanks...but a man has to earn his own pennies, even if all he's doing is saying hello to the same old faces every day."

Sarah respected Manford's desire to work. She quickly polished off a strawberry glazed donut and washed it down with a drink of decaffeinated coffee. "Speaking of work, we better get a move on. I don't want to miss the big sale."

"Oh yeah, like there's going to be a long line of people waiting to trample you down," Manford told Sarah and slapped his forehead. "The store opens at nine sharp. We have twenty minutes to beat the crowd...oh my, oh gee... twenty whole minutes...what will we ever do? I know... call the Army!"

"All right, wise guy," Sarah grinned, "grab your coat and let's hit the road."

Manford smiled. He loved teasing Sarah. But what he didn't love was that Sarah was due to go into labor at any moment. "Uh...how are the twins?" he asked. "Any sign that they might want to enter the world today?"

Sarah carefully rubbed her pregnant tummy. "Little Sarah and Little Conrad, for the moment, are very still," she informed Manford. "I'm sure my two little miracles will be kicking me in the ribs by noon."

"Speaking of our two little miracles," a voice said, "perhaps you should keep them home today."

Sarah turned and saw Conrad leaning in the kitchen doorway wearing his usual black leather jacket. "Oh, you're up. Good morning." She smiled.

Conrad fought back a yawn. "I don't want to be up, but Andrew called me. I have to get back down to the station. It seems like the drunken hit-and-run Senator Mayfield committed in our town last night is making big news."

"You didn't get home until after two," Sarah worried. "You need to rest."

Conrad walked over to Sarah and gave her a soft kiss. Manford made a sour face. "Please, I just ate," he begged.

"Yeah, yeah," Conrad fussed and hurried to the coffee pot. "Our intoxicated senator is in a world of trouble," he explained, grabbing his Charlie Brown coffee cup. "I have to go down to the station and help Andrew hold back the press."

Sarah gave Conrad a worried eye. "The man hit Mr. Hours with his car and tried to flee. That's serious business."

"It's a good thing Andrew saw the entire incident and managed to capture the senator before he could escape,"

Conrad agreed, nodding. "It's also a good thing that Mr. Hours only suffered a few bruises. It could have been worse. Senator Mayfield could be facing a murder charge instead of a hit-and-run charge."

"As well as a DUI," Sarah added, and then, "I wonder what a senator from Idaho is doing in Snow Falls."

Conrad filled his mug full of hot coffee. "Who knows? The man was so intoxicated last night he could barely walk straight. By the time he got him to the station, he passed out. According to Andrew, the guy is still in dream land."

"Who called the press?" Sarah wondered.

"I'm not sure," Conrad said. "But Sarah, you know how it is when you run someone who turns out to have a little cheese on the mousetrap. News travels fast." Conrad studied Sarah's thoughtful eyes. "Hey, I know that look. No way," he ordered. "Our twins are due any day now. Dr. Downing said you are to have no stress…you are to take it as easy as possible and—"

"I know, I know," Sarah sighed. "I know what Dr. Downing ordered, and I intend to obey his orders. That's why I'm going with Manford to O'Mally's this morning to meet Amanda." Sarah patted Conrad's arm. "Amanda and I are going to spend the morning shopping and then have lunch at the diner. Afterward I'll have Amanda drive me back home and—"

"You'll take a long nap," Conrad insisted.

"I'll take my nap and then I thought I would work on my new novel a little—twenty pages at the most." Sarah smiled into Conrad's eyes. Conrad didn't like Sarah working on a murder mystery while she was pregnant. "Twenty pages...no more, okay?"

Conrad sighed. He understood that Sarah had a deadline to meet and that her work was important. It was just that... writing a murder mystery novel while pregnant with two beautiful twin babies seemed...well, it wasn't kosher. "Sarah—"

"I'm writing humor," Sarah pleaded. "My murder mystery novel is based in an Amish setting and it's full of crazy characters. I'm not writing about a scary-looking snowman anymore...the snowman is dead, remember?"

"Well...I did read a few pages last week, and it was pretty funny," Conrad said, slowly caving in. "The Amish old man...the grandpa...sure is a nut."

Sarah felt relief touch her heart. "Wait until you see who the killer is," she teased and kissed Conrad's cheek. "Maybe it's the grandpa?"

"It wouldn't surprise me." Conrad smiled and touched Sarah's tummy with a loving hand. "Well, I better take this coffee on the road and get down to the station. I'll see you when I get home...whenever that is."

Sarah reached into the pocket of her pants. "I have my phone on me. If anything happens—"

"Send me the text and I'll have Dr. Downing to our cabin in a flash," Conrad promised.

Sarah nodded. "It's a blessing that Dr. Downing decided to move to Snow Falls. He's a wonderful doctor who is becoming a dear friend."

"He's also a nut," Conrad added. "Dr. Downing may be an excellent doctor, Sarah, but as a person…he's a certified nut."

Sarah giggled. "Yes, he is…colorful," she agreed. "Even Amanda has a difficult time handling Dr. Downing's sense of humor."

"And that should be enough to make any sane person run." Conrad kissed Sarah and walked over to the back door. "Manford, have you walked Mittens?" he asked.

"No, I let the poor dog pee herself," Manford replied and threw his arms up into the air. "Of course I walked Mittens. And as you can see, Mittens is sound asleep on her dog bed." Conrad looked into the corner of the kitchen and spotted Mittens sound asleep. "Why do you ask me that same question every morning?" Manford demanded.

Conrad shrugged. "I guess I feel the need to annoy you." He grinned and slipped outside into a soft falling snow before Manford could start fussing.

"Grab your coat," Sarah laughed. "We need to hit the road."

"Yeah, yeah, I know, I know," Manford mumbled. He walked over to the wooden coat rack standing next to the back door and took down Sarah's white coat instead of own. "Ladies first."

"Why thank you." Sarah smiled, turned off the coffee pot, checked the stove, and then had Manford help her put on her coat. "I'll go warm up the truck if you'll go check the fireplace for me, okay?"

"I already put out the fire," Manford promised as he slid on his own coat. "Yeesh, you're worse than Conrad."

"Uh…sorry," Sarah said, patting the little guy's shoulder. She walked him out into the freezing morning, feeling like a stuffed penguin waddling on fat feet. "My, isn't the snow beautiful," she said, waving at Conrad as he drove off up the street in his green truck.

Manford grabbed his arms and began to shiver all over. "Yeah, pretty…now let's get in the truck and get some heat going."

Sarah stood a moment and looked around at the white, breathtakingly beautiful world that surrounded her cabin. Snow Falls was a town that sat all alone, far north of Fairbanks and close to the arctic circle. Snow Falls was, to Sarah, a world of its own, entirely separate from the rest of the world; a treasure cove that belonged only to people who understood how to love, cherish, protect, and respect the Alaskan wilderness. For Sarah, Snow Falls also represented an escape—an escape from the life she once lived in Los Angeles; a life filled with murder and danger.

Snow Falls was clean, pure, and healing, filled with pure snow that, yes, at times was very dangerous, yet...a very old and dear friend.

"You two are going to love Snow Falls," Sarah whispered to her unborn twin babies. She touched her tummy and began walking to her truck. As she did, the cell phone in her white purse rang. "One second, Manford, let me answer this call," Sarah called out. She hurried to answer the call, expecting it to be Amanda. Instead, she saw Pete's name appear. "Hey, partner, it's a little early to be hitting the Chinese food, isn't it?" she teased.

"Not for me." Pete smiled and leaned back in Conrad's office chair. "Guess who just drove into town," he said.

Sarah froze. "No way," she said and then nearly broke out crying. "Pete, you're in Snow Falls?"

"I'm sitting in your husband's office chair as we speak," Pete laughed. "I was sent by my dear wife to buy a cabin, kiddo."

"A cabin? But...you said you would never leave Los Angeles," Sarah gasped and nearly passed out with shock. "Pete, what's going on?"

"Let's just say that I'll miss the old Los Angeles, kiddo, but the Los Angeles that I live in now...it's just sewage." Pete shoved a cigar into his mouth. "Kiddo, the private detective company we started...the cases I get...all trash. There comes a time when a cop knows when to move on. Me and the wife, we decided it was time to move on. So I shut down our business, put the house back up for sale, and traveled north to Alaska while the wife visits her sister for a week."

Sarah could barely believe her ears. "Is this a joke, Pete? Are you playing a prank? It's not nice to play jokes on pregnant women. You know I'm due to have my twins any day now and—"

"No joke, kiddo," Pete promised. "The wife ordered me to buy a cabin up here. She doesn't care what kind of cabin, just as long as I get her out of Los Angeles. She would have come with me but her sister took ill with that hip problem again." Pete stood up, walked over to the office window, and looked out at the snowy street. "I'm ready to let Los Angeles, go, kiddo, because I can't change the city back into what it used to be."

"But why Snow Falls, Pete? I thought you said you didn't like the snow."

"Well, kiddo, let Old Pete just say that he wants to be near his family…and you're his family." Pete smiled. "Besides, who knows? I may come to like the snow."

"Oh Pete." Sarah burst out crying. "Oh…I can't believe this…I…oh, I'm so thrilled," she cried. "We'll go cabin hunting together. And we'll eat at the diner, and shop at O'Mally's…and—"

"Slow down, kiddo," Pete laughed, "we have plenty of time." Pete walked back to Conrad's desk. "I called Amanda because I wanted to show up at your cabin with her as a surprise. She told me you two are meeting at a place called O'Mally's Department Store?"

"Yes." Sarah wiped at her tears.

"Meet you there," Pete promised.

"I can barely wait…and…" Sarah stopped and made a strange face. "Say, Pete, what are you doing at the station, anyway?"

"Saw a bunch of vultures—I mean, reporters—parked outside when I drove into town. Wanted to see what the fuss was all about," Pete explained. "Old habits die hard, kiddo. Unfortunately, all I got was a drunk politician being charged with a hit-and-run. Not what I wanted to put on my toast first thing in the morning."

Sarah smiled. Pete was sure going to keep Andrew and Conrad on their toes. "I have to get Manford to work, Pete. Meet me at O'Mally's, okay? Promise?"

"I promise, kiddo." Pete smiled again. "I have to meet a Mrs. Malloy after lunch. She's going to show me a few cabins."

"Oh, I know Mrs. Malloy. She's a very nice lady."

Pete studied his cigar. "New beginnings," he said and then shoved the cigar back into his mouth. "Now if I can only find a Chinese restaurant in this town."

"Oh, Pete," Sarah giggled, ending the call. She hurried to her truck and began telling a very cold and impatient Manford the great news. Manford nearly wet his pants. It was one thing having Pete live in Los Angeles…far, far away…but having the old grouch living in Snow Falls? Oh boy!

Sarah giggled as Manford perched himself inside the main entrance and began grumbling to himself. "I'll be in the snack bar with Amanda," she told him, adoring the warm and familiar atmosphere of O'Mally's Department Store. "Send Pete our way, okay?"

"And smile, you little bloke." Amanda grinned and nudged Manford with her arm. "You look constipated."

"And you look like a deranged plum in that dress," Manford fired back.

Amanda gasped. "I do not. This dress is an original all the way from London. A gift from my hubby, I'll have you know."

"Someone should have slugged the guy," Manford groaned.

Sarah giggled again. "All right, you two…let's call a truce." She pulled Amanda into a cozy, inviting snack bar. "Can you believe Pete is actually relocating to Snow Falls?" she asked in a happy voice, walking up to the snack counter. "I'm still in shock."

Amanda tossed Manford a sour eye. "This dress is an original," she fussed and stuck her tongue out at the little guy.

Manford didn't see Amanda stick her tongue at him. He was too busy checking his watch. The "Big Sale" was turning out to be a "Big Flop." The usual bored customers were the only people showing up. People with sense were hitting the town grocery store and preparing for the blizzard. But not Sarah and Amanda. No, they had to shop. "Crazy gals."

Sarah smiled and focused on the snack menu as a lovely young girl with pretty brown hair walked up wearing a red and white vest over a green shirt. "Good morning, Rachel," Sarah said in a happy voice.

Rachel O'Mally, who—bless her heart—appeared more bored than Manford, forced a polite smile to her face. Rachel was Old Man O'Mally's granddaughter. Old Man O'Mally insisted that the girl learn the business—with no special treatment, of course. No, the girl would learn the business from scratch and work her way up the ladder just like he had done. "You look like you're ready to give birth any day now, Mrs. Spencer."

"Any day." Sarah gently touched her tummy. "How is work?"

Rachel rolled her eyes. "My grandfather doesn't believe I'm ready to leave the snack bar yet," she complained. "It's the pits living with a man who is forcing me to work for him in order to pay for my college. I mean, I'm taking online college courses, you know. It's not like I'm attending some posh college." Rachel rolled her eyes again. "My grandfather is determined that I take over this store someday."

"That's not a bad life," Sarah told Rachel. "Mr. O'Mally means well. He's from the old days, so you have to give him some breathing room."

"Yeah, I know," Rachel sighed. "He took me and my mother in when my dad deserted us ten years ago. I've never been hungry or had to do without. I guess I shouldn't be complaining. It's just that I'm eighteen now and…" Rachel stopped talking and grew silent for a minute.

"And what?" Sarah asked.

Rachel lifted her eyes and looked around the warm department store. "I was going to say I want more out of life, but you know what, Mrs. Spencer? What I do have makes me very happy. I do love Snow Falls and I do love this store…I even love this snack bar. I guess I'm a bit grumpy because I didn't do so well on a test yesterday. I kind of…barely passed. Math doesn't agree with my mind."

"Oh, me neither, love," Amanda piped in. "And fractions…blimey fractions…enough to drive a woman insane." Amanda placed her purple purse down on the counter. "And the bloke who thought that teaching young minds algebraic nonsense should have been slugged. I'm a woman in her…uh…I'm a bright, beautiful woman who has never used algebra in her life."

"Tell me about it," Rachel agreed. "I use basic math to manage this snack bar."

THE MORE YOU SNOW

"Love, if a woman has a calculator, she has a best friend," Amanda pointed out and tipped a secret finger at Rachel. "That's between us."

"Our secret," Rachel promised.

Sarah grinned. "Well, I don't think we'll need math to order a decaffeinated coffee, two cheeseburgers, and a plate of hot French fries."

"No, I guess not." Rachel smiled. "Mrs. Hardcastle, what will you have? Wait…I know." Rachel took a step back and winced. "Kosher chili dogs, tater tots, a hot pretzel, and a cup of coffee, right?"

"You know it!" Amanda beamed.

"But…Mrs. Hardcastle, we just got our shipment of kosher hot dogs in yesterday…please don't eat—"

"Just keep the chili on the bun, love," Amanda told Rachel, rubbing her hands together and looking at Sarah. "This little English Muffin is in the mood to eat."

"That's what I was afraid of," Rachel moaned. "I'll…have your orders out shortly."

Sarah grabbed Amanda's arm and dragged her over to a warm booth. "Silly," she said, sitting down.

"Maybe to you Yanks," Amanda told Sarah, setting her pink coat down on the red seat. "In my family, love, you learned to enjoy food. You Yanks are very crude when it comes to food. All you do is order this or cook that and then gobble it down…no appreciation."

Sarah watched Amanda sit down and grab a pack of Mentos from her purse. "A snack before your meal?"

"Appreciation, love," Amanda teased and tossed a Mentos in her mouth. "Want one?"

"No, thanks," Sarah replied. Before she could say another word, her eyes spotted Pete stepping through the front entrance. "Pete…over here!" she called out and began waving her hand in the air. "Over here!"

Pete patted Manford on his head. "Nice seeing you again, runt."

"See this," Manford said and kicked Pete in the right shin.

"Why you little…" Pete roared and started to go for a gun tucked under the thick brown coat he was wearing. Manford let out a scared "Yikes" and took off running.

"Get back here!" Pete yelled.

"Allow me, love." Amanda giggled, jumped to her feet, and ran over to Pete before the man could shoot Manford. "This way, Mr. Trigger Happy," she told Pete, dragging the man into the snack bar. "Rachel, please add a third coffee to the order."

Pete searched the store for Manford, spotted the little man sticking his head up from behind a checkout counter. Pete pointed a finger at him. "I'll get you!"

Sarah giggled and pulled Pete down next to her. "Oh, it's so good to see you," she said, beaming, and kissed Pete on his cheek. "I can't believe you're actually in Snow Falls."

Sarah's kiss melted Pete. "Well…" he said and gently hugged Sarah. "Old Pete figured it was time to leave Los Angeles, kiddo. Besides, I want to see my two twins grow up and become mighty fine cops."

"I was thinking doctors." Sarah smiled.

Amanda sat down across from Sarah and Pete. "Listen, you old bloke, are you really moving to Snow Falls or is this one of those mid-life crisis things you Yanks go through?"

"I'm in my sixties," Pete reminded Amanda. "It's a little late to be having a mid-life crisis, don't you think?"

Amanda considered Pete's statement. "Oh…well… perhaps. But you Yanks are so blimey fruity in the head you can never tell."

Pete started to go for his gun. Sarah grabbed his hand. "There's a cabin for sale on my street, Pete."

"Yeah, that's what I was told," Pete replied, deciding it wouldn't be wise to shoot Amanda…not yet, anyway. "A three-bedroom, two-bath cabin."

"Very spacious," Sarah added. "Mrs. Pete loves space."

"That she does." Pete nodded. "But my wallet doesn't. I'm on a budget."

Sarah looked at Amanda. Amanda grinned. "Well, Pete," Sarah said, "maybe not."

"Tell that to my wallet."

Sarah steadied herself. Pete was a proud man, and she had to proceed with extreme caution.

"Sarah wants to buy you a cabin, you bloke," Amanda blurted out before Sarah could speak.

"What?" Pete asked and threw his eyes at Sarah. "What is she talking about?"

"Well…" Sarah touched her tender tummy. "Pete, my new books are really selling. And I still have all that money from my old books being turned into movies."

"The lady is loaded, and I mean loaded…L.O.A.D.E.D," Amanda pointed out.

"I know she has money. I'm not a dope," Pete barked at Amanda.

"Look, Pete," Sarah continued, "I want to do this. You deserve it."

"I'm not a charity case, kiddo," Pete barked again. "I can handle a mortgage. When my house in Los Angeles sells, I'll be able to—"

"Put that money into your retirement fund," Sarah begged and touched Pete's arm. "Pete, I'm going to buy you a cabin, whether you like it or not," she continued, forcing her voice to sound stern and stubborn. "You're my family, and families love each other…so…so…there!" Sarah felt like a third grader arguing with her mommy.

"I see," Pete said, folding his arms and watching Manford sneak back to his duty station. "So your word is final, huh?" he asked. Sarah carefully nodded her head yes.

Pete looked into Sarah's stubborn eyes. Sarah didn't want to buy a cabin out of pity or charity—no, the woman's actions originated from a deep, undying love that only Pete understood; a love that had developed over the course of many years between two cops who became family, father and daughter. "I won't let you—"

"I want you to have the cabin that's for sale on my street," Sarah insisted. "Money isn't an issue, Pete. I want you as close to me as possible…please." Sarah placed Pete's hand on her pregnant tummy. "I want you to be around and watch my baby boy and baby girl grow up."

Pete felt his heart break. "How…can a man say no to that?" he asked in a choked voice and turned his head. "Must be something in the air…"

Sarah felt a tear drop from her eye and hugged Pete. As she did, Conrad stepped through the main entrance, had a few words with Manford, and then made his way into the snack bar. He was covered with snow.

"Conrad?" Sarah asked in a worried voice. "Is everything okay?"

"Oh sure," Conrad said and sat down next to Amanda. "Thanks for leaving a half-eaten donut on my desk, Pete," he complained. "The ants loved it."

Pete grinned. "You better get used to me hanging around the station house," he warned. "And speaking of the station house, why aren't you on the job?"

"Because Senator Whitfield is dead."

"Dead?" Sarah gasped.

"Heart attack," Conrad explained and waved a hand at Rachel. "Coffee and cheeseburger, please. No mayo—I don't want to have to arrest you."

"I'll add a gallon of mayonnaise," Rachel fired back and rolled her eyes. "Mrs. Spencer, you better put a muzzle on that guy before I slap him with a broom."

"Yeah, yeah," Conrad said and focused back on Sarah. "Senator Whitfield woke up for a few minutes and began threatening everyone—and then he had a heart attack. We tried to save him, but by the time Doc Downing arrived... too late."

"Oh, that's too bad," Sarah said in a sad voice.

"Well, the guy was up there in his years," Conrad pointed out. "Who knows what kind of health he was in? And he was a bit overweight."

"My doctor said I have a heart of a forty-year-old," Pete told everyone. "Men in my family have always lived into their nineties."

"Is that a good thing?" Amanda teased Pete. Pete went for his gun but Sarah stopped him. Amanda grinned. "You old bloke, you know we love you."

"Anyway, I knew you were here and decided to stop by," Conrad continued. He smiled at Sarah and then looked at Pete. "I guess seeing you again isn't all bad."

"Funny," Pete barked at Conrad and then added, "We're going to be neighbors, so keep running your mouth, funny man."

"Neighbors?" Conrad asked but was quickly interrupted by his cell phone. "It's Andrew, I better take this." Conrad answered the call. "Yeah, Andrew?"

"We have a slight problem," Andrew told Conrad, standing in his office wearing a confused expression on his face.

"A problem?"

"Senator Whitfield's body is missing," Andrew explained. "Doc Downing said he had the body placed in the morgue at the hospital…routine stuff…but the body isn't there anymore. Doc Downing said he is having the hospital turned upside down…so far…no body."

Conrad ran his left hand through his black hair. "Are you kidding me?"

"Wish I was."

"What is it?" Sarah asked.

"Senator Whitfield's body is missing from the hospital morgue," Conrad whispered just loud enough for Sarah, Amanda, and Conrad to hear. "Okay…I'm on my way to the hospital."

"The press is at the hospital," Andrew warned.

"Great," Conrad said and ended the call. He looked at Sarah with tired eyes. "So much for our early morning date, huh?" he asked.

"Maybe I should go with—" Sarah began to offer.

"No," Conrad stated in a stern tone. "Sarah, I can handle a missing body."

"Maybe so, but this old cop is going to tag along," Pete informed Conrad. He patted Sarah's hand and stood up. "I'll watch after your husband," he promised.

"More like give me a headache," Conrad griped. He stood up and called to Rachel to make his coffee to go.

"Don't push it, boy," Pete warned.

Conrad grinned. "In this town?" he asked. "What else is there to do?" Conrad bent over the booth and kissed Sarah. "I'll be home when I can, okay? You just make sure to take your afternoon nap."

"I will," Sarah promised, feeling a funny sort of tingling in her gut. Sure, a man was dead and a body was missing, but for some reason Sarah felt the situation was… well…funny.

The snowman wearing the leather jacket and chewing the candy cane was dead—forever; the darkness had been destroyed. What Sarah didn't know as she waved goodbye to Conrad and Pete was that she was about to embark on her very last murder case—a very funny case that would end her career as a cop and begin her career as a full-time mother.

"Well," she told Amanda, "let's eat and then get to our shopping, huh?"

Amanda watched Conrad and Pete leave through the front entrance and then smiled. "You know how we always talked about this wonderful store and how much we love it?"

"Yes." Sarah smiled back.

"Now we're living our dream, love," Amanda said in a soft, warm, secure voice. She patted Sarah's hand in a way that let the pregnant woman know that everything was going to be okay. "Now, where are my kosher chili dogs? This English muffin is hungry and ready to shop. The stack of pancakes, omelet, turkey bacon, biscuits and gravy, toast, and cereal didn't fill my tummy up."

2

Sarah strolled over to a wooden dress rack sitting on the warm brown carpet that Old Man O'Mally went to great lengths to keep clean. The carpet covered the women's clothing area while a glossy hardwood floor covered the men's. Sarah preferred the carpet.

"This is a pretty dress, and it's twenty percent off," she told Amanda, studying a white long-sleeved dress with pink and blue polka dots. Amanda, who was chewing on a candy bar, made a barfing sound. "I take that as a no, then?" Amanda nodded. "Okay…okay." Sarah backed off from the dress and began searching through other designs.

"You know, love," Amanda told Sarah, walking her eyes around the nearly deserted store, "if it wasn't for the approaching snowstorm, we would be having a little competition."

"Are you complaining?" Sarah asked, studying a blue dress with little red and white candy canes sewed onto the fabric.

"Oh, I just miss the…thrill of a sale, that's all," Amanda explained. She polished off her candy bar and began working on a strawberry slushie. "It's really no fun fighting over a dress when you don't have a thousand elbows shoved into your rib."

"Old Man O'Mally may shove his elbow into your rib if you spill your slushie on this carpet. You're not even supposed to take food or drinks out of the snack area, remember?"

"Oh, pooh," Amanda fussed, "a woman needs her energy to shop."

Sarah grinned. "Five kosher chili dogs, three plates of hot French fries, two cheeseburgers, three hot pretzels, a candy bar…and now a slushie. I'd say that's plenty of energy." Sarah nudged Amanda with her elbow. "Who is the pregnant one, anyway?"

Amanda blushed a little. "So I have high metabolism," she told Sarah, taking a sip of her slushie. "Little body…needs lots of food."

"Tell me about it," Sarah teased and held up the blue dress with candy canes for Amanda to examine. Amanda studied the dress and made a *take it or leave it* face. Sarah decided to take it and tossed it into a green and red shopping cart. "Can you believe that Pete is actually leaving Los Angeles?" she asked, taking her eyes back to the rack of dresses. "I would have never imagined Pete would be able to leave L.A. Mansion Lane…the beach…downtown…the canyons…"

"Sounds like you miss Los Angeles," Amanda offered.

"Oh, I'm just like Pete. I miss the old days…before Los Angeles really took a nosedive," Sarah confessed. "Now the city is consumed with criminals that run city hall. The moral foundation of the city has become a corrupt fountain of tyranny and poison."

"So the author speaks." Amanda smiled.

Sarah blushed. "Sorry. I guess sometimes I do let the writer in me speak."

"Well, the writer is speaking the truth," Amanda confirmed. "Every major city in the United States is corrupt…and my dear London has also become, as you say, a corrupt fountain of tyranny and poison. People have become…diseases," Amanda said as she worked on her slushie. "Not all people, but the majority. It's disheartening to see how people are deserting their moral obligations to honor sin."

"I know," Sarah sighed. "I've been thinking about what type of world my twin babies are going to grow up in. What type of world they're going to have to fight."

"A world that will try to brainwash them into believing immortality is good and morality is evil."

"Just like the Bible teaches," Sarah sighed again. "But, as you said, not everyone is bad. There's still good people in this world, June Bug, and those people make a difference." Sarah smiled at Amanda and nudged the woman with a loving elbow. "You make a difference."

"I cause people to take aspirin, love," Amanda giggled.

"Well, at least you're helping the pharmaceutical companies stay in business." Sarah laughed and looked around O'Mally's with adoring eyes. "As ugly and immoral as this world has become, we still have our O'Mally's. We still have our little Alaska town, and that's enough for me. Do you want to know why?"

"Kosher chili dogs and a tiny little man standing at the front entrance?" Amanda suggested.

"Well, that...but..." Sarah reached out and hugged Amanda. "I have you."

"Oh, I love you, too," Amanda melted and gently hugged Sarah.

Sarah felt a tear drop from her eye as Amanda hugged her. "We almost died at the hot springs. We both were infected with a very deadly virus. But we made it through, didn't we?" Sarah put her hands on Amanda's shoulders. "You've always been there for me, from the very first day I moved to Snow Falls. You saved Conrad and me from that deranged model and—"

"Love," Amanda said and quickly wiped Sarah's tears away, "I love you, too."

Sarah looked deeply into Amanda's loving eyes, hugged the precious woman, and then wiped more tears away. "Back to shopping?"

"You bet." Amanda beamed and then spotted a short, grumpy-looking old man who was nearly bald approaching from the north side of the store. "Uh-oh," she said and ducked the slushie behind her back.

Sarah lifted her eyes and spotted Old Man O'Mally hurrying toward them, using a wooden cane to assist him, wearing his usual brown suit. The old man did not look happy; in fact, Sarah noticed, the old man appeared very scared.

"Mr. O'Mally, are you all right? You look a little pale."

Old Man O'Mally glanced around to make sure no other shoppers were present. In all truth, his store only had four shoppers, and two of those shoppers were Sarah and Amanda; the other two, both old men, were wandering about the men's clothing area searching for new long johns. "You are in a very delicate position, Mrs. Spencer." He spoke in a voice that struggled to sound calm rather than grumpy and mean. "And I would have called your husband…but I do not wish to make a scene."

"A scene?" Sarah asked, studying Old Man O'Mally's eyes. An eccentric cousin in Michigan made a scene. A crazy criminal infecting people with a deadly virus made a scene. An insane kid from Los Angeles who targeted Sarah in Oregon made a scene. A fruity model building creepy snowmen wearing leather jackets made a scene. A criminal

FBI agent made a scene. A mafia boss made a scene. A British sniper bent on revenge made a scene. A crazed man who took a pregnancy game show hostage made a scene. All of the killers Sarah and Amanda faced in the past made a scene—including the Back Alley Killer and his daughter. What type of scene could poor Old Man O'Mally be worried about making? Did he knock over a rack of socks?

"Mr. O'Mally, please explain," Sarah said.

"This way," Old Man O'Mally whispered and then shot Amanda a sour eye. "No drinks outside of the snack area, you…and stop eating all of my kosher chili dogs. I can't keep them in stock."

"I could take my business elsewhere," Amanda warned.

Old Man O'Mally nearly passed out. Amanda was his number one shopper, besides Sarah. The two women practically kept his store in the green. "Now, now, let's not be drastic. There are exceptions to the rule," he fumbled and then made a few grumbling sounds under his breath. "Have your…slushie."

"Thank you, I will," Amanda said in a pleased voice.

Sarah sighed. Amanda was too silly. "Mr. O'Mally, what is the problem?" she asked, grabbing her purse—a purse hiding a gun.

"This way," Old Man O'Mally said and led the two women to the back of the store and into a large storage room holding rows and boxes, wooden shelves packed with smaller boxes, wooden racks holding dresses, sweaters, shirts, and other clothing items that had not been put out onto the main floor yet, a few old television sets (Old Man O'Mally refused to sell flat-screen TVs and insisted that the old televisions were better—Sarah and Amanda happily agreed), a few furniture items, and other merchandise that sat about like bored children. Old Man O'Mally hung a right and walked to a row of eight-foot-tall wooden shelves, went three rows down, and then hung a left.

"There," he said in a creepy voice and raised his right finger. "Look and see for yourselves."

Sarah stepped up beside Old Man O'Mally and saw a man who appeared to be sitting against the wooden wall, leaning forward with his arms slouched on the floor as if he were either asleep or passed out.

"I see him," she whispered.

"I believe the man is dead," Old Man O'Mally whispered back. "I yelled at him several times but he hasn't moved an inch."

Amanda tugged her head over Old Man O'Mally's shoulder, spotted the body, and then took a sip of her slushie. "Anyone you know?" she asked him.

"Of course not," Old Man O'Mally fussed under his breath. "No one is allowed in this storage room except employees. As of today, I have no storage boys on the clock. I had a small delivery this morning and came back here to process the merchandise personally because… business is a little slow."

"The sale flopped, you mean," Amanda corrected. She took a sip of her slushie and studied the body. "Hey, you awake or dead?" she called out, nearly scaring Old Man O'Mally out of his skin. "Hey…wake up!"

Sarah studied the man who was slumped over. He was wearing a very fancy gray suit. The man also appeared to be a…bit overweight. "Senator Mayfield?" Sarah whispered.

"The missing dead guy?" Amanda asked.

"Could be," Sarah said and calmly opened her purse and pulled out a Glock 19. "Stay here," she said, handing Amanda her purse, and cautiously approached the body. "Senator Mayfield?" she called out even though it was clear that the man was dead.

"Oh, this is spooky," Amanda said in an excited voice. "A missing dead body turns up at O'Mally's. Real horror movie stuff…and with a snowstorm approaching, too."

"This is far from amusing," Old Man O'Mally snapped at Amanda, watching Sarah reach the body. "Is he dead?" he yelled.

Sarah studied the slouched-over man and then used her left hand to check for a pulse. The man was cold all over and…very much dead. "No pulse…body is cold," she called back. "This man is dead."

"Then what in the world is he doing in my storage room?" Old Man O'Mally demanded.

Sarah shrugged her shoulders as her eyes fell onto the thick gray hair resting on the dead man's head. The hair appeared damp with melted snow; the fancy gray suit also appeared damp. "I'm checking the pockets for identification. June Bug, call Conrad."

"Oh, I'll go call your husband," Old Man O'Mally snapped and hobbled away with his wooden cane, fussing up a storm. "Lawsuit...dead body...storage room."

"Oh, stop fussing, you old coot," Amanda called out, grinning as she walked up to Sarah. Ordinarily—especially after all the killers she and Sarah had tangled with in the past—Amanda would have been very upset and scared. But for some strange reason she felt completely at ease. Who knew why? Dead bodies weren't exactly a walk through a field of strawberries.

"Senator Mayfield?" she asked.

Sarah handed Amanda her gun and began checking through the dead man's pockets. She came up empty-handed. "No identification. But according to Conrad's description of Senator Mayfield, this could be the missing dead man."

"How many missing dead senators does Snow Falls have, love?" Amanda asked. She polished off her slushie and set the empty cup down on the wooden shelf to her left. The aisle was tight, which meant that if a killer was lurking about, he—or she—would be forced to attack from behind. Amanda calmly turned her body around to face the opening of the aisle. "What now?"

Sarah began checking the dead body for any signs of violence. "Body appears clean," she said and asked Amanda to help her stand up. Being pregnant with twins meant that she couldn't bounce down onto her knees and shoot up like a rocket the way she once did. "All we can do is wait for Conrad and Pete to show up."

"Works for me," Amanda agreed, handing Sarah back her gun. She looked around. "How do you suppose someone got a dead body back here without being seen?" she asked.

"Good question. Come on." Sarah exited the aisle, leaving the dead body alone, and walked to a set of double metal doors hugging the back wall. "All deliveries come through this door," she explained. "These two doors are the only way into or out of this storage room." Sarah pointed to three powerful metal bolt locks. "The first bolt secures the top of the doors...the second bolt the middle...and the third bolt the bottom."

"Not to mention that." Amanda pointed up at a metal gate that Old Man O'Mally pulled down over the two metal doors every night. "No one is getting into this room unless they use a torch."

Sarah nodded her head. "Old Man O'Mally did say he had a delivery this morning." Sarah studied the doors and then walked her eyes around the silent storage room. There were obvious places where a killer could be lurking, but her gut insisted that the warm storage area was clear of danger. Yet, Sarah did feel she was being watched. "Hello?" she called out.

No sooner did Sarah yell than a blast of white smoke exploded in the aisle the dead body was on. "Alvin the Great is never to be seen!" a man yelled in a talented magician's voice. "Away we go!"

Sarah hurried over to the aisle and began slapping at the smoke. "You…stand still!" she yelled, spotting a shadowy figure picking up the dead body. "Stand still…hands in the air!" She coughed, raising her gun into the air. "Don't make me shoot you!"

"Alvin the Great is never to be seen!" the man yelled and then, to Sarah's shock, he vanished right before her eyes, taking the dead body with him.

"Uh…love." Amanda coughed as she fought smoke away from her face. "Who was that?"

Sarah lowered her gun and slowly backed away from the smoke-filled aisle. "I have no idea." She coughed, searching the smoke with watery eyes. "Whoever it is must still be in here."

Amanda opened her mouth to agree but then felt a cold blast of air and spun around just as the metal double doors burst open. By the time she reached the doors, "Alvin the Great" had escaped into the snowy woods standing behind O'Mally's. "Well, isn't this just peachy. I just might need another kosher chili dog."

Conrad looked at Sarah and Amanda like the two women had literally lost their minds. "Seriously?" he asked.

"What do you think, sparky?" Amanda fussed. She grabbed Conrad's face and slung it toward the two metal doors Alvin the Great had escaped through. "Do you think we're making this tale up? Shake the fudge out of your brains and eat some spinach like Popeye! Blimey, you Yanks are impossible!"

Conrad twisted his face away from Amanda. Before he could say anything, Old Man O'Mally stepped forward and began shaking his wooden cane at him. "I did a check and I'm missing certain items. I have been robbed. I want the thief captured! Do you hear me!"

"Yes, sir," Conrad said, holding up his hands to wave off the wooden cane before Old Man O'Mally whacked him a good one. "What exactly was stolen, sir?"

"Old Fourth of July fireworks merchandise...smoke bombs...fireworks," Old Man O'Mally said.

"Is that all?" Conrad dared to ask.

"No, that isn't all, you smart mouth," Old Man O'Mally snapped, forcing Sarah to turn her head to hide her amusement. "Clothes...a black winter coat, to be exact, a set of white sheets, rope...three hand mirrors...and...oh, I'll make you a list." Old Man O'Mally shook his cane at Conrad and then wobbled out of the storage room like a wet hornet.

"Fussy little guy." Pete grinned, leaning against the back wall and chewing on a cigar. "I like him."

"You'll get used to Old Man O'Mally," Conrad promised with a roll of his eyes and then focused back on Sarah and Amanda. "Honey—"

"Conrad, Amanda and I saw a man steal the dead body," Sarah assured her weary husband.

"That's right, you…blimey bloke," Amanda growled at Conrad. She snatched a candy bar out of her purse and went to town. "Some bloke who called himself 'Alvin the Great.'"

"'Alvin the Great'?" Pete asked. "Can't say that name rings a bell. I can make a few calls and check the streets all the famous magicians walk on. Who knows? We may get a lead."

Conrad rubbed the back of his neck. "Sarah, Senator Mayfield's family is going to arrive in Snow Falls within the next three hours. Needless to say, the family is not… pleased that the body of their dear loved one is missing. I can't tell them that some weird magician stole it. Andrew will shoot me if I do."

Pete chuckled. "This is a strange one," he admitted.

Sarah took Conrad's arm and hugged it. "I'm sure you'll solve this dangerous case." She smiled. "Gather all the clues, examine all the evidence, and then…get tickets to a magic show."

"Very funny," Conrad replied, rolling his eyes, and then decided to smile. "I guess it is funny. A missing body...a guy who appears to be a magician...and an approaching snowstorm. Snow Falls might be small, but it's never boring."

Sarah snuggled up to Conrad. "It's time for my afternoon nap. Drive me home."

"I'll take you," Amanda piped in. "And I'll be staying with you until the magician is caught. Not that I'm scared," she quickly added, "but...dead bodies are a little creepy." Amanda eased up to Sarah. "I'll kick Manford out of his bed. The little runt can sleep on the couch."

"Good thing I got a room," Pete chuckled again. "Conrad, we better get back down to the station."

"Yeah, I guess," Conrad agreed. He kissed Sarah's forehead. "But first I better get the list Mr. Grumpy is making me."

"How about checking the woods?" Amanda asked, pretending to talk in a tough cop's voice even though she just admitted she wanted to stay at Sarah's cabin because a dead body was floating around somewhere out in the snow. "Check for boot prints in the snow and all that."

"Wind has erased the prints, genius," Conrad fired at Amanda. "The weather is getting worse. Snowstorm is almost right on top of us."

"Oh," Amanda replied and then simply shrugged her shoulders and polished off her candy bar. "As you Yanks say, you can't blame a gal for trying. Saw that saying on an old black-and-white movie I was watching last night."

Conrad growled. "Someone get her out of here."

Amanda quickly grabbed Conrad's hand and bit it. Conrad let out a painful yell. "Ready to go, love?" she asked Sarah.

Sarah giggled to herself and touched her pregnant tummy. "You two are impossible."

Conrad rubbed his wounded hand and then began going for his gun. Pete darted over to him. "Calm down, boy," he laughed, preventing Conrad from shooting poor, little, innocent Amanda. "We have a case to work on. Come on." Pete tipped Sarah and Amanda a wink and then dragged Conrad out of the storage room.

"One of these days…!" Conrad yelled as Pete dragged him away.

Amanda grinned. "Nice husband you have, love. Tastes like chicken…or, as I read in a book about a woman who owns a peach bakery in Georgia, tastes like a whole bunch of turkey, yes sir and yes ma'am," Amanda finished in a thick, cheesy Georgia accent.

"Let's keep you away from Georgia," Sarah laughed. She grabbed Amanda's hand and pulled her out of the storage room, and they headed for the store's exit. When they reached Manford, he was sitting on a small stool by the doors reading an old *Jughead Double Digest*. Sarah winced as she explained to the little guy that Amanda was going to be staying at the cabin for a few days as a guest.

"That means you're on the couch, you little runt," Amanda told Manford, slapping him in the back of the head. Why? Oh, just for the fun of it. Amanda loved to get the small man riled up.

"Hey! Watch it," Manford yelled, dropping his comic book. "That's a classic 1988 edition." Manford jumped off the stool and looked up at Amanda with red, glaring eyes. "Why, I ought to slug you!"

"You couldn't slug the top of a slug, you little runt!"

"Oh yeah…well…take this!" Manford ran up to Amanda and kicked her right in the shin. Amanda let out a loud howl and began hopping around on one leg. Manford didn't wait around. He took off on his short little legs and ran for the back of the store—where he would wait just long enough for the coast to clear.

"You two," Sarah sighed, grabbing Amanda's arm and pulling her friend out into the heavy falling snow.

"I'll kill him!" Amanda promised, limping to her snow-covered truck. "I'll do worse than kill him. I'll tie him up and feed him to a hungry grizzly bear! No…better yet, I'll hide all of his *Archie* comic books. That'll teach that little runt to kick me."

"Well, June Bug, you did start that fight," Sarah pointed out, raising her eyes up to a low, stormy, dark gray sky. The sky appeared threatening, yet Sarah found comfort in the storm. While the world south of her was loud, polluted, dangerous, and immoral, she was standing in a completely different world that was clean. Special. A world that belonged only to her, a world created by snow. "Look, let's just drive back to the cabin, have a snack, and then I'll take a nap while you do your Sudoku."

"Any more cake left from yesterday?" Amanda asked in a pouty voice, reaching the driver's side of her truck.

"Two slices. Conrad and Manford really like coconut cake."

"My slices," Amanda pouted, climbing into her truck and getting some heat going.

Sarah waited a minute and then tapped on the passenger side window. "Uh…June Bug?"

"Oh…of course, love!" Amanda jumped back out into the snow, ran around to Sarah, and helped her best friend climb up into the truck and get comfortable. "Better?" Sarah nodded. Amanda smiled, ran back to the driver's side, climbed in, and got the truck moving. "I guess we can come back to O'Mally's tomorrow, huh?" she asked, easing through a snowy parking lot filled with a few frozen trucks. "The sale still has four more days."

Sarah smiled and began warming her hands up. "I would like to go back and get that blue dress I found," she said, attempting to create a normal conversation instead of focusing on the strange events that had taken place in the storage room. "I really liked that dress."

"Well, love, candy canes are cute…but on a blue dress…a little…loud." Amanda began to explain her position as she reached the road in front of O'Mally's, carefully turned right, and began driving back toward Sarah's cabin. Deep down, Amanda wanted to turn left and visit the small business part of town that held a handful of fast food restaurants—especially the new Chick-Fil-A. But Sarah needed her rest and the health of a dear friend who was pregnant with precious twins was more important than a Chick-Fil-A Chicken Deluxe sandwich. "Your colors are pastel, love. You're not a loud person. Now, if the candy canes had been sewn onto a softer blue, I would have personally bought the dress for you."

Sarah listened to Amanda fall into a fashion lecture and leaned her head back. It was going to be a long ride back to her cabin. But so what? Sarah adored Amanda and didn't mind her best friend going on and on about a dress that was too "loud" for her skin complexion and hair. Besides, deep down, Sarah knew Amanda had better taste in clothing than she did. Sarah was simple; Amanda was complex.

"So I won't get the dress." Sarah smiled as Amanda turned onto her street. "Goodness…the plows really need to pay my street a visit again. The snow has really gotten deep."

"Hold on, love!" Amanda yelled. She threw her truck into four-wheel-drive and hit the gas. Sarah grabbed the dashboard and held on for dear life as Amanda bulldozed the growling truck down the snow-soaked street and then swung into her driveway like a madwoman. "Old Bertha can be mean when she wants to be!" Amanda cried out in victory.

"Are you trying to send me into labor?" Sarah asked, breathing hard. "June Bug…I saw my life flash before my eyes at least ten times…and my street isn't very long."

Amanda grinned. "Old Bertha needed to stretch her legs."

"Stretch her legs…nearly send me into labor," Sarah began fussing. She heaved herself out of the truck and wobbled up to the back door of her cabin, blinking away the snowflakes on her eyelids. "Nearly send me into labor," she continued as she opened the back door and stepped into a warm kitchen…only to be greeted by a dead body slumped over the kitchen table—the same poor dead body that had been slumped over in the back storage room of O'Mally's.

Sarah immediately froze, her eyes locked on the body, and then went for her gun. "June Bug!" she yelled and began waving her hand at Amanda.

Seeing the alarm in Sarah's flailing hand, Amanda hauled butt out of her truck and hurried through the snow. When she reached the back door and spotted the dead body, she looked at Sarah with confused eyes. "Alvin the Great strikes again," she whispered.

Sarah began searching the snow for any signs of footprints or drag marks but came up empty. "He could be inside the cabin," she whispered.

"Think we should go inside?" Amanda whispered back, staring at poor Senator Whitfield.

Sarah hesitated. "Listen, you," she yelled into the cabin, "I'm a pregnant woman with a gun...and that's bad medicine...so don't make me shoot you!"

"My friend is also a retired cop, and she can shoot a wing off a fly a mile away, so you better stop playing games you...bloke!" Amanda added and then waited for Alvin the Great to show himself. When silence appeared, she tossed a worried eye at Sarah. "We can drive back into town?"

"No, I need to call Conrad," Sarah said and very carefully stepped into her kitchen. "Stay close, June Bug," she whispered, working her way toward the telephone hanging beside the refrigerator.

"I am close," Amanda whispered, holding onto to Sarah's left arm and peering at the dead body with nervous eyes. "If that dead body moves...I'm screaming."

Sarah tossed an eye at the body and then focused back on the telephone. "Let's remain...rational," she stated, grabbing the phone and calling Conrad's cell phone. "Yes, it's me. I've just arrived home with Amanda and found Senator Whitfield's body in our kitchen... Okay...hurry... but drive safe, the snow is getting deeper." Sarah hung up the phone and looked around the kitchen. "Conrad and Pete are on their way."

"What do we do until they arrive?" Amanda gulped. Sure, she didn't feel that the situation held any life-threatening danger, but a dead body…creepy, especially since Alvin the Great began playing Bingo with it. Now Amanda kept seeing the body somehow come back to life like a creature in an old horror movie. "Too much pizza before bed," she whispered, holding onto Sarah's arm.

"We wait," Sarah answered Amanda. She hurried to close the back door and then dared to check the dead body for a second time. "No signs of violence…no identification…body is cold…hair and clothes are wet from the snow." Sarah studied a pool of water that had formed on the floor around the chair where Alvin The Great had placed Senator Mayfield's body. Unfortunately, the snow she and Amanda had tracked in made it impossible to detect any other tracks.

"Hey, where is Mittens?" Amanda asked, suddenly noticing that the family dog was missing.

Sarah could have kicked herself. "Mittens! Mittens, girl, come to mommy!" she called out.

Mittens trotted into the kitchen from the living room carrying a dog bone in her mouth—a new dog bone that neither Conrad nor Sarah had bought for the dog. Mittens happily went to her doggy bed, lay down, and began gnawing on the bone. As she did, Sarah heard the window in Manford's bedroom open…and then…a few seconds later…close. Sarah gripped her gun, grabbed Amanda's hand, and crept back to Manford's bedroom only to find it empty. She did, however, locate a set of snowy boot prints.

"What in the world is going on?" she asked Amanda, staring out Manford's window, watching a shadowy figure vanish into the snowy woods behind the cabin. "Who are you...what do you want?"

Amanda stepped beside Sarah, looked out at the snow, and then sighed. "I need some cake," she said and started back for the kitchen. There was no sense in trying to solve a murder case on an empty stomach. Besides, the kosher chili dogs she had polished off at O'Mally's hadn't exactly filled her tummy. Murder has a way of doing that—especially a strange murder.

3

Conrad watched a young volunteer paramedic haul Senator Mayfield's body out into the snow on a wobbly stretcher. The body, which was now resting in a black body bag, seemed like a curious hot potato rather than a dead man.

"It's clear that this 'Great Alvin' person knows you," he told Sarah, feeling cold, heavy snow striking his face as evening approached.

"Alvin the Great," Sarah gently corrected her husband, sitting at the kitchen table sipping on a hot, decaffeinated coffee. "And yes, I agree. This…body thief…seems to have chosen me."

Andrew, who was standing out near a black and red ambulance with Pete, waved a hand at Conrad. "We're going to the hospital to stand guard over the body," he called over the howling, icy winds. "Meet us there!"

Conrad waved back at Andrew and then closed the kitchen door. "How are you feeling?" he asked Sarah in a concerned voice. "You missed your afternoon nap."

Sarah shot a curious eye at Amanda. Amanda had her head shoved in the refrigerator searching for a snack. "The bloke asked me, love...I couldn't lie," Amanda called out from the refrigerator. She grabbed a box of half-eaten pizza and hurried to the kitchen table. "Ah, cheese pizza. Just what the doctor ordered."

"Give me a slice. I'm starving," Conrad told Amanda.

Amanda rolled her eyes. "Get your own food, you greedy snot."

Sarah grinned. As tired—and confused—as she was, whenever Conrad and Amanda were in the same room together, they always made her smile. "I wouldn't try to take a slice of pizza," she warned Conrad.

"Fine," Conrad fussed, stomping over to the refrigerator and snatching out a pack of turkey deli meat. "I'll make myself a sandwich...healthier anyway."

"Deli meat still has cholesterol, love," Amanda informed Conrad and winked at Sarah.

"So does your mouth," Conrad fired back. "Someone should put a public health warning label over that thing." Amanda rolled her eyes, stuck her tongue out at Conrad, and then focused on her pizza. Why let a bloke like Conrad make her lose her appetite? "Listen," Conrad told Sarah as he worked on fixing a quick sandwich, "there has to be a rhyme and reason to this guy's madness."

"I agree," Sarah said with a nod. "However, I have yet to come up with a clear and identifiable theory that holds water." Sarah took a sip of her coffee. "Conrad, we need to begin with Senator Mayfield and find out what he was doing in Snow Falls in the first place. What's his connection to this town?"

Conrad slapped a piece of pepper jack cheese down onto a slice of wheat bread. "I don't know yet. And by the way, Senator Mayfield's family won't be arriving on schedule," he said. "This storm shut down all the roads south of us."

"You sound disappointed?" Sarah asked.

"I am disappointed," Conrad confessed. "I want Senator Mayfield's family to sign for his body and leave town. Being stuck with the man's body means we have more time to—"

"Lose the body again. Yes, I know," Sarah said. "However, the delay gives us time to search for answers," she carefully pointed out as a strong gust of icy wind shook the warm cabin. "My, this storm is getting very powerful."

"I checked the generator. We're good," Conrad assured Sarah and hurried to finish his sandwich. "Pete made a few calls. He didn't find anyone on the magician circuit named Alvin the Great."

"Well, it's clear this mystery magician knows Senator Mayfield. We need to grab a shovel and see what we can dig up on the senator," Sarah emphasized. "Have Pete call some of his contacts."

Conrad took a bite of his sandwich. "Pete is on the same page as you," he told Sarah with a mouthful of food.

"Oh, gross, don't talk with your mouth full, you rude bloke," Amanda cried. "Where are your manners? You Yanks…gross!"

Sarah grinned again. "Uh, June Bug…you're talking with a mouth full of pizza."

Amanda touched her mouth. "Oh…sorry, love." She blushed and hurried to swallow her food.

Conrad rolled his eyes. "Does she have to stay here?"

"Yes, she does," Sarah replied and rubbed her tired eyes. "Can you two please try to get along?"

"I would rather bury that bloke up to his neck in an ant bed," Amanda pointed out.

"I'd rather bury your mouth in an ant bed!" Conrad fired back.

"Don't make me stick your face in a snow blower!" Amanda fired back and shook her fist at Conrad.

"Please," Sarah begged, holding back laughter, "will you two act like adults for a minute? We have a serious case on our hands and need to brainstorm."

"He started it," Amanda pouted.

"Did not," Conrad insisted. "Too bad your husband didn't take you to London with him."

"Too bad you didn't stay in New York, you smelly bloke!"

"I don't smell!" Conrad quickly sniffed at his left arm pit to make sure.

Sarah sighed. "Both of you…enough," she pleaded. "We need to focus. Now, Conrad, you help Pete dig up whatever you can on Senator Mayfield. I'll jump online and start digging around and—"

"You're going to bed," Conrad ordered Sarah. "You missed your afternoon nap, remember? Dr. Downing insisted you take your naps."

"I'm too wired up to sleep," Sarah insisted. "Besides, I'll be sitting down in my own home. It will be no different than sitting down to check an email."

"Sarah—"

"Honey," Sarah cut Conrad off in a loving voice, "a dead body was placed in our home. I want answers." Sarah touched her pregnant tummy. "Our twins could be in danger, so please don't expect me to be able to lay down and sleep."

Conrad let out a heavy sigh. His wife had a point. "Just as long as you're sitting down."

"Of course," Sarah promised. "I will ensure that I rest at all times."

"Well...I guess sitting at the computer isn't much different than sitting at the kitchen table drinking a cup of coffee." Conrad walked over to Sarah, kissed her forehead, and made his way to the back door. "Okay, I'll be with Pete if you need me. In the meantime, I've locked all the windows and secured the front door and—"

"And I have my gun and Manford will be home shortly." Sarah smiled. "Rachel is driving him home after his shift."

Conrad rubbed the back of his neck. Leaving Sarah alone with a deranged magician on the loose didn't sit well with him. However, this "Alvin the Great" guy didn't seem to be dangerous—yet. Instead, it seemed to Conrad that the man was trying to make a point of some kind. What kind of point? Conrad didn't know—yet, the answers would become clear in time. In the meantime, Sarah had her gun, and the woman was a mean shot.

"Look, I don't know how that guy got into our cabin...so keep an ear out, okay?" he pleaded.

"Will do," Sarah promised.

Conrad tossed a weary eye at Amanda. Sure, Amanda was a royal pain in his backside—a wart on his side—but the woman was a loyal friend and a brave soul that he respected; a woman who had become a sister to him. "Watch my wife very carefully, Amanda. I'm leaving her in your hands."

Amanda nodded. "With my life," she promised. Conrad gave Sarah a loving smile and escaped out into the freezing snow. Amanda hurried to the back door. "It's just you and me, love," she said, locking the door with a quick hand. "I guess I'll...bake a cake while you start searching for Alvin the Great...and eat the rest of my pizza while the cake is baking."

Sarah watched Amanda approach the pantry door. "We have tons of cake mixes in the pantry," she promised. "Between Conrad and Manford, I can't keep enough of them in the cabin."

Amanda opened the pantry door and studied the interior, taking in a deep breath of flour, spices, and canned goods. "Love?" she said in a curious voice.

"Yes?"

Amanda kept her eyes peeled on the interior of the pantry. "Why did Alvin the Great leave that dead body in your kitchen? I mean...it's very curious, isn't it?" Amanda locked her eyes on a wooden shelf holding lines of brown cake boxes. "That bloke could have killed us...he was inside the cabin. Instead, he gave Mittens a chew bone. It doesn't make sense to me."

"Well," Sarah answered in a thoughtful tone, "I've been wondering if this 'Alvin the Great' person is trying to lead me to something."

Amanda stepped into the pantry, grabbed two cake boxes, and then retrieved a container of chocolate frosting along with a tub of red and green sprinkles. The snow was putting her into a Thanksgiving/Christmas mood that felt warm and cozy, even if there was a strange, deranged magician on the loose. Amanda—for some reason she couldn't really put her finger on—didn't feel that the unknown man was a threat or a danger. "I suppose that could be true," she answered Sarah, enjoying the warm atmosphere of the pantry.

Sarah stood up from the kitchen table—which took some doing—rubbed her tender tummy, stretched her back, and then studied the back door. "June Bug, I'm wondering if Senator Mayfield was murdered," she said, throwing a hidden theory out into the open air.

Amanda slowly closed the pantry door with her right foot. "But Conrad said he died of a heart attack."

"I know." Sarah rubbed her back as little Conrad let out a mighty kick. "Goodness!" Sarah cried out.

"What?" Amanda nearly freaked out. She threw her loot down onto the kitchen counter and ran to Sarah. "Did your water break…is it time? I'll call Dr. Downing…where is his number?"

Amanda began to run for the phone. Sarah quickly grabbed the panicked woman by the collar of her dress. "June Bug…calm down…little Conrad gave me a strong kick, that's all." Sarah let go of Amanda's collar and tummy. "I guess I woke him up…go back to sleep…it's okay."

"Oh blimey, I almost had a heart attack," Amanda complained and wiped sweat from her forehead. "Little Conrad…when you're born, remind me to tie your legs together."

Sarah grinned. "I have a feeling Little Conrad is going to be a mess," she told Amanda. She patted her friend's shoulder and wandered into a warm and cozy living room holding an inviting fire in a cobblestone fireplace. "All right, Alvin the Great, let's see what I can dig up," she said, forcing her mind to start functioning as a cop as she sat down at a polished wooden desk holding a computer. "June Bug, I forgot my coffee!"

"Blimey," Amanda fussed, her heart still racing, and then rushed Sarah her coffee. "Love, do me a favor," she said, setting Sarah's coffee down on the desk. "When you do go into labor, don't tell me. I don't think my nerves can handle the excitement."

Sarah looked up at Amanda. "How did you react when you went into labor with your son?" she asked in a curious voice.

Amanda walked over to the fireplace, took a log from a metal wood bin, and shrugged her shoulders. "Oh, my hubby was at work and I was in the flat alone," she explained. She tossed the log into the fire and began warming her hands. "My water broke when I was standing in the kitchen peeling potatoes. I managed to get next door to Mrs. Notforth. Mrs. Notforth, who is a mother of seven sons, drove me to the hospital in a calm way that kept me at ease." Amanda turned away from the fireplace and smiled at Sarah. "Hours later, my son was born…a healthy, beautiful boy."

"Was it…painful?" Sarah dared to ask, wondering what delivering not one but two babies was going to feel like.

"Well…" Amanda winced. "Love, childbirth is…painful… and it takes a woman's body time to heal…but the joy of giving birth far outweighs the pain we feel for a few hours." Amanda walked over to Sarah and took her best friend's hand. "The joy of bringing a precious, innocent life into the world, the joy of becoming a mother—even though you become a mother the day of conception—far outweighs any physical pain a woman endured during her hours of delivery. You'll see."

Sarah looked up at Amanda with love and gratitude. "Just be there to hold my hand, okay, June Bug?"

"And let that bloke from New York take my place, no way!" Amanda teased. She gave Sarah a warm hug and wandered back toward the kitchen to start baking a cake.

Sarah touched her pregnant tummy, whispered a prayer of love, and then went to work. The first thing she did was begin an intensive search that focused on past and present magicians who had performed in and around the Los Angeles area. Alvin the Great, judging by the man's voice, appeared to be in his early to mid-thirties. However, Sarah wasn't sure if the man was disguising his voice or not, which was why she took her search back as far as 1980.

"Let's see…" she whispered, searching past performances that had been held at popular hot spots as the icy winds began to howl and scream outside. "No Alvin the Great to be found…" Sarah rubbed her chin, thought for a few minutes, and then decided to change directions and check arrest reports. "Maybe if I can create a suspects list, I'll find a name that I can match to the list of magicians."

Using a skilled and trained detective mind to operate her fingers, Sarah began checking all public arrest reports. After an hour of searching through arrest profiles that didn't seem to match Alvin the Great, she sat back in her leather office chair, rubbed her eyes, and sighed. "This guy could be anyone…" Feeling exhaustion begin to take its toll, Sarah slowly started to allow her mind to call it a day when a sudden idea struck like lightning.

"Hey…of course," she said in an excited voice. She pulled up Senator Mayfield's public profile and checked to see if the man had any children. "One son…Raymond A. Mayfield."

"Any breakthroughs, love?" Amanda asked, walking into the living room carrying a pot of decaf.

"I'm not sure." Sarah rubbed her sore neck and then took her coffee. "Thanks, I need a refill."

Amanda leaned down and studied the glowing computer screen. "Raymond A. Mayfield?" she said and then her eyes grew large and white. "Hey…could that bloke be Alvin the Great?"

"I don't know. I'm going to run Raymond A. Mayfield and see what I can dog up. Who knows?" Sarah took another sip of coffee. "This might turn out to be a very interesting case, June Bug…very interesting indeed."

Alvin the Great (a.k.a. Raymond A. Mayfield) walked into a warm living room lined with log walls that appeared to be very old. The old logs didn't bother Alvin. He enjoyed the rustic aspects of life. He was a man who had been raised in Cincinnati, Ohio until the age of seventeen and then relocated to Boise, Idaho after his old man decided it was time to start a new career when the state of Ohio began sniffing around his financial records. Alvin wasn't thrilled when he ended up living in what he called "the Boonies," but he soon grew to love the rugged landscape of Idaho.

He attended college while his old man dived into politics and ended up majoring in theater, where he met a friend who was an amateur magician. Alvin thought his new friend was a real dork for having an interest in phony magic acts, but after a while, mostly over a girl who attended his friend's acts, Alvin became interested in the illusion of magic. Over the next ten years, he dedicated himself to perfecting his magic act. He performed in major shows all across the world under the name Rusty Smoke, deciding to change his name to Alvin the Great in order to give the famed detective Sarah Garland-Spencer a clue to his true identity. Why? Because Alvin needed Sarah's help trapping a deadly killer; a killer who was a mystery to Alvin.

"You certainly must have understood my message," he said, sitting down on a brown chair with a bowl of hot vegetable beef soup. "I hope so."

Alvin locked his eyes in a comfortable fire playing inside of a stone fireplace and listened to the winds howl and scream outside. Snow Falls, he knew, was a very rural town that the outside world rarely touched. The town consisted of people who understood the hidden dangers whispering underneath the howling and screaming winds —people who knew the dangers of deadly temperatures and deep snow. While Alaska surely held unimaginable beauty, the land also held unseen dangers that could swallow a person whole.

"I'll need to be careful," he said, taking a bite of soup, careful not to drop any on the thick brown sweater that matched his wavy brown hair. "I'll call the famed detective tomorrow and see what data her mind has collected."

Yes, Alvin knew that at the age of thirty-five, he still talked like a theater dork and still dressed like a nerd, but so what? It wasn't like he was engaged to some beautiful princess from some foreign country. No way. Alvin was a single man who—even though famous on stage—couldn't get a date to save his life. Why? Because in reality he was still the same old "Nerdy Alvin" he had been in his early school years; the same old Nerdy Alvin the bullies had beat up and shoved into snowbanks.

"I was going to show everyone by running for governor. Dad was going to help me…but now he's dead."

Alvin closed his eyes. "Being Rusty Smoke is lonely. Becoming governor of Idaho…surely a fair damsel would have attached herself to my lonesome heart. Now it's up to

Alvin the Great to bring justice to the death of a fallen man."

Alvin sighed. Yeah, he was a dork, but Senator Mayfield had been his dad, and even though the man had been corrupt, it was the duty of a son to bring justice to the person who killed him.

"Alvin the Great must not fail," Alvin whispered. "Also, it never hurts to have a famed detective on your side...I hope."

Alvin opened his weary eyes and studied the warm living room belonging to a cabin he had rented. The cabin sat on the far edge of Snow Falls, but that didn't matter. Alvin had a snowmobile, a pair of skis, his health, and a determined heart to help him battle the approaching snowstorm. Besides, the tedious work of hauling his old man's body around was over—or so it seemed.

"I'll rest for the night and then allow tomorrow to bring me answers," Alvin said. He glanced at the coffee table holding a cell phone and sighed. "On nights like tonight I wish I had a girlfriend to talk to...even all of my old friends have deserted me. Alvin the Great is...alone. Alas...all the great suffer...alone."

Sarah had no idea that Alvin the Great was sitting alone in a rental cabin hungering for companionship. No, she was sitting before her computer reading all about Raymond A. Mayfield. "Rusty Smoke was his stage name before he retired two years ago," she told Amanda. "Raymond A. Mayfield became a hit at the age of twenty-eight. He spent five years traveling the circuit performing famous disappearing acts."

"Disappearing acts?" Amanda asked, cuddling a brown plate holding a large piece of chocolate cake decorated with green and red sprinkles.

"Every magician has their specialty, I guess," Sarah answered and took a bite of her own cake. "My…very moist. I believe this is the best cake you've ever baked, June Bug."

Amanda grinned. "Well, I did have the kitchen all to myself," she teased a little.

Sarah lifted a curious eye. "Are you implying that I am a distraction?"

"Would I dare carry out such a terrible tragedy, love?" Amanda gasped.

Sarah nodded her head. "Yes."

Amanda giggled. "Well…you do have a tendency to distract me when I'm baking just a tiny little bit."

"I do talk a little too much, don't I?"

"Only when you're fussing about your hubby." Amanda giggled again. "Last time I baked a cake you were sitting in my kitchen fussing about how your dear hubby called you fat."

"Well…Conrad didn't really call me fat. He said that my dresses might seem a little big after our twins are born,"

Sarah pointed out and then sighed. "I suppose I didn't take his words very well, did I?"

"My cake came out flatter than a pancake, love." Amanda grinned.

"Sorry."

"Don't be sorry," Amanda told Sarah. She took a bite of cake and grinned. "You're married to a Yank. I have to allow you room to fuss. Now...what about this bloke who likes to disappear?"

"Oh...uh, well, according to this profile he gave up his stage show at the age of thirty-three and moved back to Boise, Idaho after his dad was reelected state senator."

"Fishy," Amanda stated.

"Also, according to this profile, Raymond A. Mayfield was going to run for state governor in the next election."

"Which isn't too far away," Amanda pointed out.

Sarah nodded, took a bite of cake, washed the cake down with some decaffeinated coffee, and continued. "Official public campaigning begins in a few months."

"You mean the mudslinging begins in a few months." Amanda rolled her eyes. "Whenever election time arrives, you can bet your pretty muffin that you're going to start seeing a bunch of so-called civilized blokes reduce themselves to name-calling rats. And the worst part is, people actually vote for those rats...like any blimey bloke in a suit cares a fart about them. An elephant's muddy butt would make a better…" Amanda caught her tongue. "Sorry, love, I can't stand politicians. They make my stomach turn."

"It could be that Senator Mayfield was killed for political purposes," Sarah pointed out. "We have to figure out why the man was in Snow Falls, and I have a feeling Alvin the Great is trying to help us."

"Why doesn't that bloke just knock on your door and tell you face to face?" Amanda asked.

"Good question. Perhaps he's scared of someone…or some people?" Sarah suggested. "Or maybe there's another reason? I don't know." Sarah took another sip of coffee and listened to the snowstorm outside barrel down on Snow Falls. "This storm isn't going to make it easy for any of us to move about. The plows will clear the streets tomorrow until one o'clock, and after that, everyone is on their own once the snow piles back up."

"Snowmobiles and skis." Amanda smiled. "I don't mind when the snow shuts down our lovely little town. I like being snowed in with a cup of hot coffee and a warm book."

Sarah walked her eyes to the living room window. "I like being snowed in, too, June Bug, but now isn't exactly the best time for a snowstorm." Sarah touched her tender, pregnant tummy. "Conrad checked the snowmobile out in the shed—we're okay—and I called Dr. Downing and he assured me his snowmobile is in good working condition and—"

"Love, it's all right," Amanda promised in a soothing voice. "Even if Dr. Downing isn't able to reach you, I've been trained, remember? I'm a confident midwife."

"But what if there's…complications?" Sarah worried, keeping her eyes on the living room window. "June Bug, what if my twins need immediate medical attention…need to be flown to a larger hospital and—"

"Every test has shown that your precious twins are amazingly healthy, love," Amanda soothed Sarah's worried mind. "Those two little runts sleeping in mommy's warm Jacuzzi right now are going to be born very healthy." Amanda rubbed Sarah's shoulder. "You're having the same thoughts I had before my son was born… all the what-ifs that crawl into your mind at the last hour. And you know what?"

Sarah took her eyes away from the living room window and looked up into a warm, loving, tender face. "What?"

"That's perfectly normal." Amanda smiled. "But Los Angeles, my dear friend, put your mind at rest because this English Muffin has the situation under control…assuming there is a chance that Dr. Downing might not be able to reach you, that is." Amanda squeezed Sarah's shoulder with a loving hand. "Now, what do you say we let Alvin the Great rest for tonight and play a game of Monopoly."

"Oh, Monopoly always makes me sleepy and"—Sarah paused, saw Amanda grinning, and sighed—"It's time for my bed."

Amanda nodded just as Manford burst through the back

door fussing up a storm. "Stupid plows…Rachel couldn't get to our street…had to walk the entire way!"

"The little runt is home." Amanda grinned, helped Sarah stand up, and walked into the kitchen.

"Stupid plows didn't clear our street," Manford fussed, kicking snow off his boots and shaking snow off his coat. "I nearly froze!"

"A midget Popsicle," Amanda teased. She poured herself a fresh cup of coffee and took a sip. "Nice, hot coffee…you should try some," she told Manford.

Manford shook his little fist at Amanda. "Don't push it, lady!" he yelled, snatching a brown muffler off his head. He looked at Sarah. "Why are you up? You should be resting!"

"I know, I know," Sarah assured Manford. "I was conducting some research—"

"About the dead man, right?" Manford rolled his eyes. "Yeah, I should have known. Old Man O'Mally…I should punch that old fart for involving you…in your state. I mean, the twins could arrive at any second now!" Manford marched over to Amanda and stole her coffee away. "Hey, not bad," he said.

Amanda lifted her right foot and kicked Manford in his butt. "You bloke."

"Hey…watch it…you nearly made me spill my coffee!"

"My coffee, you mean." Amanda grinned, feeling grateful that Manford was home. Sure, the little guy was tiny, but he held the heart of a giant warrior. "I baked a cake. Want a slice?"

"What kind of cake?" Manford asked, sitting down at the kitchen table. "Mittens, come say hey to daddy…Mittens," he called out. Mittens, who was sound asleep, perked her ears up, opened her eyes, and then dashed over to Manford. "That's my girl," Manford laughed and began rubbing Mittens' ears.

Amanda smiled at Sarah. Manford loved Mittens. "Chocolate cake with green and red sprinkles is the dessert of the hour," she spoke.

Manford froze. "Did you say…green and red sprinkles?" Amanda nodded. "I love green and red sprinkles. Green and red sprinkles rock my socks."

"Then I'll make your slice of cake extra large," Amanda promised and set out to cut Manford a slice.

Sarah wobbled over to the kitchen table and sat down across from Manford. "So…besides the body…anything interesting happen at work today?"

"Nah…store was dead because of the storm," Manford explained. "Old Man O'Mally pulled me away from front door duty and had me vacuum, sweep, and mop and then help Rachel close down the snack café. But"—Manford reached into his coat pocket and pulled out a check —"today was payday," he said, beaming. "Now I can get the twins that set of blankets I've been wanting to get them."

"Manford, we have money and—" Sarah began to object.

"Your money…I need to earn my money," Manford cut Sarah off in a stern but loving voice. "I want to buy the twins that set of blankets with money I earn…money Uncle Manford earns."

Sarah felt a tender smile touch her face. Oh, how she loved her little Manford. "Okay…and…thank you. I know the twins will love the blankets."

"The twins will be too busy pooping and gassing to love anything," Manford grinned, "but someday they'll know Uncle Manford loves them." Manford looked at Amanda. "Oh, hey, by the way, look outside the back door."

"The back door?" Amanda asked. Manford nodded. Amanda shrugged, walked a plate of cake over to Manford, and then hurried to the back door and opened it. Two green and red O'Mally Department Store bags were sitting in the heavy falling snow. "Hey, shopping bags!" she yelled in an excited voice. She dragged the bags inside and carried them into the kitchen.

"One bag is for you and the other bag is for Sarah…I kinda watched you two looking at the dresses earlier," Manford explained.

"Oh, you shouldn't have," Sarah said.

"Yes, the little bloke should have!" Amanda beamed and yanked a green dress with little snowmen on it out of one of the bags. The green was soft and matched Sarah perfectly. "Oh, this must be for you, love!" Amanda handed Sarah the dress and then pulled a white dress with pink and blue roses on it out of the second bag. "My... it's...beautiful," she gasped. "I didn't see this dress—"

"Your dresses were in the back." Manford smiled. "Old Man O'Mally let me have them for forty percent off. I hope you like them. I kinda took a guess at what you two might like, you know?"

"I love my dress," Sarah promised. Amanda nodded and kissed Manford on his cheek. Manford blushed. It was great having a family.

What the little guy didn't know was that far away, a lonely man was sitting by himself eating soup and wanting a family as well. Also, what Manford didn't know was that a deadly killer was loose in the snowstorm, determined to kill the lonely man—determined to kill Alvin the Great.

4

Conrad wiped sleep out of his eyes as he wandered into the kitchen. "Good morning," he yawned as his ears took a second to listen to the snowstorm outside. "Man, this storm is really growing," he said in a worried voice.

"Coffee is on the counter and your breakfast plate is in the oven," Sarah told Conrad, sitting at the kitchen table with a notebook and pencil in hand.

Something in Sarah's eyes told Conrad that his lovely wife had been up awhile—and doing some serious thinking. He poured himself a cup of coffee and retrieved a brown plate from the oven that held pancakes, turkey sausage, biscuits, gravy, and an egg omelet. "A meal fit for a king," he told Sarah and sat down across from her. "You've been cooking."

"I couldn't sleep," Sarah confessed. "I put Amanda's and Manford's breakfast plates in the oven, too. They'll eat when they wake up." Sarah studied the back door with careful eyes. "I checked on Manford a few minutes ago. He's in a coma on the couch. A bomb couldn't wake him up."

"I don't think it's a bomb that you're worried about," Conrad pointed out, yawning again. He took down some hot coffee, feeling like a wrinkled piece of worn-down laundry in his black leather jacket. "You've been thinking about Raymond A. Mayfield."

"Yes, I have," Sarah told Conrad in a deep, thoughtful voice. "I've been wondering why he led me down this path. It's obvious, at least to me, the man wanted me to discover who he is...but why?"

"Pete is working on that," Conrad assured his wife.

"If I know Pete, he's tucked under a ton of warm blankets snoring up a storm right now. The man can go days without sleep, but when's he down...he's down for the count." Sarah lowered her eyes to the pad of paper she was holding. "Raymond A. Mayfield isn't married...no children...mother died when he was five...raised by his dad..." Sarah tapped the pencil she was holding against her chin. "Senator Mayfield left Ohio after the state began investigating his recycling business...that was eighteen years ago..."

"Could be the man made some enemies along the way?" Conrad suggested, taking a minute to wake up before he tore into the delicious breakfast Sarah had cooked.

"Raymond A. Mayfield was preparing to run for governor

next year. He was being backed by Senator Mayfield," Sarah continued. "There does seem to be a political attack behind this, don't you think?" Conrad nodded. "Has Dr. Downing come across any new findings?"

"Heart attack is still the cause of death," Conrad explained. "However, I did find out last night, after taking a very ugly phone call, that Senator Mayfield's family isn't exactly… kosher. I wanted to tell you the news, but you were sound asleep."

Sarah perked up her ears. "Feed me the news."

"Well," Conrad said, swallowing a bite of turkey sausage, "Senator Mayfield married a woman named Mona Jamison four years ago after divorcing his second wife…a woman by the name of Alice Grates, if I remember right." Conrad washed down the turkey sausage with coffee and continued as the storm howled and screamed into a snow that was falling in thick, vicious, torrential streams. "Mona Jamison has two daughters and a son from a previous marriage." Sarah nodded, listening closely. "But, here's the kicker. Mona Jamison is almost twenty years older than Senator Mayfield…and she was married to the man Senator Mayfield beat out as senator…a man who turned up dead, by the way."

"Oh, that is interesting," Sarah told Conrad as she continued to tap the pin against her chin.

"Mona Jamison and her son, a guy named Tom Jamison, are the ones determined to reach Snow Falls."

"Not the daughters?"

71

"The two daughters are married and living in New York and Virginia. Tom Jamison is still single…never married…works for Boise as the city attorney." Conrad took some more coffee down. "I don't know how the man still has his job. He has a rap sheet longer than my arm full of DUIs."

"Well, when you have friends in the right places," Sarah pointed out.

"Tell me about it," Conrad replied in a sick voice. "Mommy dearest sure takes care of her son."

Sarah grew silent for a minute and listened to the storm. She began wondering about Mona Jamison. "Conrad, who is the man running against Senator Mayfield in the next election?"

Conrad grinned. Sarah was sharp. "A man by the name of Ryan Elderson," he answered. "Some guy who moved up to Boise from California two years ago."

"Is Ryan Elderson…friendly…with Mona Jamison?"

"Pete is working on that," Conrad explained. "Ryan Elderson is only a few months younger than Mona Jamison, by the way…a real scumbag, too."

"Oh?"

Conrad took down some more coffee. "Ryan Elderson is the type of guy who wants to destroy the American Constitution and turn our country into a dictatorship. Mona Jamison isn't far behind him."

"I read that Senator Mayfield's political views weren't exactly patriotic," Sarah pointed out.

"That guy was a scumbag, too." Conrad glanced at the back door. "It was too late for Andrew to run the rental cabins. That will be the first thing we do today and see if we can track down this Alvin the Great."

"Assuming he rented a cabin," Sarah pointed out.

Conrad looked back at Sarah. "You don't believe this guy is hiding out?"

"No, I don't." Sarah shook her head. "I believe Mr. Raymond A. Mayfield needs my help and that you're most likely going to contact the cabin rental agency and find out that he's legally rented a cabin." Sarah put down her pad of paper and pencil, grabbed her cup of decaf, and then touched her tummy with her left hand. "The twins were really up and kicking this morning. I think they're about as sick of decaffeinated coffee as I am."

"Speaking of our twins, I want you to stay indoors today and rest," Conrad ordered. "The plows couldn't make it out today, Sarah. I'll be traveling by snowmobile and—" Before Conrad could finish, the kitchen telephone rang. "That's probably Andrew. This storm has crippled all cell phone service." Conrad stood up and answered the call. "Hello?"

"May I speak to the grand detective who captured the Back Alley Killer?" Alvin asked Conrad in a pleasant voice. "Please tell her that Alvin the Great is wishing to converse with her and that I do apologize for calling at such an early hour."

Conrad tossed wide eyes at Sarah. "It's Alvin the Great," he stated, "and he wants to speak to the...grand detective who caught the Back Alley Killer."

Sarah stiffened a little at the mention of the Back Alley Killer. Yes, the killer was dead, and so was his daughter... but the name still sent chills into her heart. "One second..." Sarah struggled to stand up and waddled over to the telephone. "Hello, Mr. Mayfield, this is Detective Sarah Spencer. How may I be of assistance?"

"Ah, so you know who I am. Perfect," Alvin stated in a pleased—and relieved—tone. He slowly poured coffee into a brown coffee cup with a white bunny on it and then walked over to a window, careful not to stretch the telephone cord attached to the kitchen phone too far, and studied the snowstorm. "Before we speak, Detective, please allow me to state...if ever so redundantly...that I did not kill my biological parent."

"Dr. Downing has confirmed that the cause of death was a heart attack," Sarah stated and shrugged her shoulders at Conrad. She needed to get inside Alvin's mind and find out who the man was.

"Perhaps that is true...and perhaps it isn't," Alvin said cryptically. "Detective, my...well, let's call him Senator Mayfield for the time being, shall we?" Sarah said sure. "Senator Mayfield and I were never what a person would call...close. The man was a horrible drunk and a crook. Honesty and integrity were his enemies."

"Isn't that true for all politicians?" Sarah asked.

Alvin let out an amused chuckle. "Yes, I do suppose it is. However, when one is assigned as your biological parent, it saddens the heart to see the truth revealed. However, I was a spunky child that managed to stay ahead of the game by reading and writing and making sure I knew when to hide in my wall locker when the school bell rang."

Alvin continued to study the storm, wondering if he dared to venture out into the snow or should stay inside. "When Senator Mayfield...shall we say...fled...the state of Ohio and moved me to Idaho, I was not pleased. However, in time, I came to love the wilderness. The wilderness, I found, was not judgmental and accepted me for who I was. I felt free and unconstrained...fearful of bears rather than humans. But I digress..." Alvin took a sip of coffee. "You are probably wondering why I'm playing with a dead body?"

"Well...yes," Sarah confessed. "Mr. Mayfield, why don't you come and speak with me in person?"

"Because my life is in danger," Alvin stated. "The people who killed Senator Mayfield will surely kill me—if given the chance. And, rest assured, my dear detective, those people will not rest until I am sleeping six feet under next to Senator Mayfield." Alvin turned away from the window and studied the warm kitchen. "Also," he added, "I have other reasons for wanting to remain…unseen. Alvin the Great must never be seen…not until it is time."

Sarah felt a headache approaching. "Mr. Mayfield, my twins are due to be born any day now. I don't have time for games."

"And I don't have time to die," Alvin retorted in a firm yet respectful voice. "My dear detective, I returned to Idaho hoping to become a strong political figure at the suggestion of Senator Mayfield himself. I foolishly believed that the hallowed man was attempting to mend our bruised relationship…I was sorely misled in my judgments." Alvin felt a touch of bitterness enter his heart. "I now have no desire to enter the political circus. My desire is to go back to being a magician…and I intend to do so with, shall we say, a real bang—one that will make the world forget all about Rusty Smoke and say hello to Alvin the Great."

Sarah bowed her head. "Mr. Mayfield, there's a snowstorm outside. All I have to do is trace the number you're calling from and track your location. The storm has crippled all cellular service, so I know you're calling from a landline. Please don't make this any more difficult than it needs to be. Please…just cooperate with the law and help us in locating the people you believe killed your father."

"I'm afraid that isn't possible, my dear detective," Alvin told Sarah and kicked himself a little. "While it may be true that Alvin the Great is no superhero, he is a man hungering for justice. Senator Mayfield was a louse, but he was also my…dad. Justice must be carried out in the name of…uh…justice." Alvin kicked himself again. "I also have to ensure justice is carried out in order to resume my career. Unless the villains are destroyed, Alvin the Great will always have to hide in the shadows."

"Shoot me," Sarah whispered to Conrad, rubbing her eyes. She then shook her head. "All right, Mr. Mayfield, can you at least tell me what you and Senator Mayfield were doing in Snow Falls and what happened the night he hit Mr. Hours?"

Alvin glanced down at the dorky green sweater he was wearing. The sweater had a black magician's hat sewn onto the front with a pair of rabbit ears sticking out. Oh well, such was the life of Alvin the Great. "I suppose the words 'running in fear' come to mind," he told Sarah. "Senator Mayfield was running from the people who wanted to kill him."

"Dr. Downing's medical opinion is that Senator Mayfield died from a heart attack," Sarah pointed out.

"Perhaps…and perhaps not."

Sarah felt her patience wearing thin. "Care to explain?" she asked.

"Perhaps Senator Mayfield was poisoned…that has to be the case," Alvin told Sarah in a secretive tone. "Senator Mayfield never had heart problems."

"Dr. Downing will run an autopsy," Sarah assured Alvin. "He'll find out if any…poison…killed Senator Mayfield."

"We shall see," Alvin agreed. "In the meantime, I shall say that I saw Senator Mayfield strike the poor man who was crossing the street. It was my desire to help the poor man but I feared my enemies were close by and fled the scene on foot. For that, I'm guilty, my dear detective." Sarah heard bitterness rise in Alvin's voice and waited. "Senator Mayfield was deserting me, I'm afraid...like a rat deserting a sinking ship. He was quite shocked when I appeared in your snowy little town and feared that I had been followed."

"Keep talking."

Alvin took a sip of coffee. "I drove Senator Mayfield into town in his own truck in order to put some solid substance into his body. The fella was very...shall we say...juiced. I managed to get him to eat a little bit of food at your local diner and then, as we were departing and preparing to return back to his rental cabin, the man shoved me down onto the snow and escaped in his truck, striking an innocent man in the process. He was soon apprehended by your local badges and arrested...and then he died."

"Who was he running from, Mr. Mayfield?" Sarah asked.

"Not yet," Alvin told Sarah in a careful voice. "If I confess the true faces hiding behind the dark masks, I may make a mistake I...may not live...to regret. No, it is better if I give you a clue."

"A clue?"

"A wife cannot be trusted when her heart is not full of light," Alvin stated.

Sarah listened to Alvin's words and then asked: "Senator Mayfield's wife?"

"Yes." Alvin nodded. "That snake is out of her hole again and slithering about. You are indeed very sharp." Alvin put down his coffee. "In the meantime, I will be out in the snow today. Perhaps I will make a visit to the hospital?"

"Mr. Mayfield, I still have questions that need to be answered. For instance—"

"I've said enough for now," Alvin told Sarah. "My dear detective, I am not your enemy. I will be in touch. Until then, departing causes me great pain. Farewell…for now."

Sarah handed Conrad the phone. "I don't know whether to call the little white men with butterfly nets on the guy or feel sorry for him," she stated in a frustrated voice. "'Alvin the Great'…good grief."

Conrad put down the telephone. "I'll give Andrew a call and track this clown down, okay?"

"You may track Alvin the Great down," Sarah warned, "but when you do, he may vanish right before your eyes." Sarah looked toward the kitchen door and listened to the snowstorm and began wondering who was truly wandering around in the snow unseen and unheard.

———————

Conrad stood outside a closed wooden door that led into a small, lonely morgue that was currently holding two bodies. One of the bodies belonged to Old Lady Mills, a ninety-eight-year-old woman who was found dead in her bed from what Doc Downing called "Natural Causes." The second body belonged to Senator Mayfield—and Conrad wasn't about to let Alvin the Great steal the man's body again. Of course, Conrad had no reason to believe Alvin the Great would steal Senator Mayfield's body again, but who would have thought it would have been stolen in the first place?

"You know, Pete," he said, taking a sip of hot coffee, "we located the cabin Raymond A. Mayfield was staying at. The place was empty except for a fire burning itself out in the fireplace. Alvin the Great could be anywhere."

Pete heard frustration in Conrad's voice. "Well, if he shows up here, we'll catch him," he said, speaking with a chewed-up cigar in his mouth. "Right now, we don't have much to go on. All we can do is wait."

"I wish Dr. Downing would perform the autopsy already," Conrad fussed.

"Dr. Downing, from what Andrew explained, is busy upstairs taking care of those two fellas who got hit in the head with a fallen tree limb." Pete tossed his thumb up toward the ceiling. "Before that, it was those three hunters who were found half frozen to death. And then there was Mrs. Mills and—"

"Yeah, yeah, I know, Dr. Downing has his hands full," Conrad complained. He studied his coffee and then glanced at Pete. "Pete, your contacts haven't found anything?"

"Breadcrumbs," Pete sighed. "Mona Jamison, as far as we can tell, is clean except for a few bumps here and there that don't add up to much. The woman has been keeping herself in the clear."

"And nothing on Senator Mayfield…" Conrad leaned his head back against the closed door. "Pete, there has to be something."

"We're still digging, Conrad." Pete chewed on his cigar for a few seconds. "We're still digging on Tom Jamison and Ryan Elderson. It takes time. My people still have regular police work to do, you know."

"Yeah." Conrad took a sip of coffee. "My eyes are on Mona Jamison's first husband. The guy ended up sleeping in a bathtub holding a plugged-in hairdryer. I doubt he killed himself."

"The coroner marked Albert Jamison's death as suicide," Pete pointed out. "The man's body was cremated shortly afterward. Not much to dig at from there."

"Which leads us right back to Mona Jamison." Conrad watched Pete put his cigar into the front pocket of his gray overcoat and then pull out a candy bar. "We have to make sure Dr. Downing performs an autopsy on Senator Mayfield."

"Mrs. Jamison is demanding no autopsy be performed," Pete reminded Conrad. He opened his candy bar, took a bite, and then studied the deserted corridor. The hallway was lonely and cold, lined with a depressing yellowish gray tile and dark brown walls that felt bitter to Pete. Of course, Pete reminded himself, he hadn't visited a morgue yet that didn't have a depressing hallway attached to its body. Hospitals went to great lengths to ensure their front lobby, offices, waiting rooms, and other areas were decorated with life—yet, underneath the hospital…desertion and depression. "What the eyes can't see," he whispered.

"What?" Conrad frowned.

"Oh, nothing," Pete answered and worked on his candy bar. "Mona Jamison made a call to the Alaska governor's office, you know? Dr. Downing may be prevented from carrying out an autopsy."

"Andrew hasn't heard anything from the governor…yet." Conrad studied the hallway. "Time isn't on our side, Pete."

"But the weather is." Pete grinned. "And who is to say that Dr. Downing has to obey any official orders from the state capital?" Pete polished off his candy bar. "Conrad, according to the latest weather report, that storm outside isn't going anywhere for a few days, and by the time it does leave, we'll be buried under so much snow it'll take weeks to dig us out." Pete glanced up and down the hallway and continued. "This storm is keeping Mona Jamison at a safe distance. The woman is trapped in Anchorage, and the governor is currently in Maryland on some type of 'official' meeting. Maybe time isn't on our side…and then again, maybe it is. But one thing is for certain: The snow is definitely on our side."

Conrad took some coffee down and let Pete's words sink in. "You may be right, Pete. Maybe the storm is keeping Mona Jamison at bay, but that doesn't change the fact that a killer could be loose. As far as we know, this Alvin the Great guy could be the killer." Conrad finished off his coffee. "And if he's not the killer, then the real killer is most likely loose in our town, hiding. He could be anywhere."

"If Senator Mayfield was murdered," Pete warned Conrad.

"My gut is telling me the man was murdered."

Pete took his cigar back out, tossed it into his mouth, and let out a troubled breath. "Yeah, me, too…but I still want to wait for an official autopsy report to confirm what my gut is telling me." Pete chewed on his cigar for a few seconds. "Conrad—" He was cut off when a flash of thick white smoke exploded into the air. "It's…him!" Pete began coughing, spit out his cigar, and went for his gun. "Guard the door!"

Conrad felt the taste of smoke mingled with tear gas begin filling his eyes and nose. He quickly covered his mouth. "Tear…gas," he yelled, using his right hand to yank out his gun from a hidden shoulder holster.

Pete began waving at the white smoke as another smoke bomb exploded, turning the hallway into a thick bay of impenetrable fog. "Guard…the…door," he coughed, desperately covering his mouth and eyes. "Conrad…don't

—" Before Pete could finish his words, a hard hand reached out of the smoke holding a mean, short, wooden baseball bat. All Pete saw before his world went black was the baseball bat flying right at his head. "Lights out, cop!"

"Pete!" Conrad yelled, searching the smoke for his friend. "Pete…talk to me!" Conrad would never admit how he felt about Pete, but deep down, Pete meant the world to him. Sure, Pete was cranky and always smelled of cigar smoke, but the man was a great cop and closer than a brother. If anything ever happened to Pete, Conrad would never be able to forgive himself. "Pete!"

"Time to sleep, cop," a voice hissed and smacked Conrad in the head with the baseball bat. Conrad saw stars and then dropped into a heavy, dark dream filled with white smoke. "Now, time to get the body and get out of here."

Tom Jamison, who was supposedly trapped in Anchorage with Mona Jamison, rushed through the closed door wearing a gas mask, hurried through a small office, and then entered a cold room lined with stainless steel walls. Three stainless steel tables sat in the middle of the room. The middle table was occupied with the body of Old Lady Mills. The table to the left was empty…and the table to the right held nothing but a crumpled up white sheet.

"What?" Tom asked with wide, shocked eyes. He ran to the table, snatched up the sheet, and then threw his eyes around the cold room. "No…this can't be!" Tom searched the cold room with panicked, angry eyes and then fled the hospital, escaping through the same emergency side door that was old, rusted, and scarcely utilized by any of the hospital staff. The door led Tom into an icy, metal stairwell that held a single flight of stairs that took him to the first floor and led him out to the back of the hospital where he had left his snowmobile parked in the snowy woods. "He has the body…again…" he hissed. He furiously jumped on the snowmobile and tore loose.

From the roof of the hospital, Alvin watched Tom depart. Then he proceeded to escape with Senator Mayfield's body, using the powerful snowstorm as cover.

"Alvin the Great must never be seen," he said, lugging the dead body down a slippery fire escape. "I fear…I must not let the authorities have you back…for now." Alvin cautiously climbed down the slippery fire escape, holding the dead body over his right shoulder, using every bit of strength his body could muster, and then hurried off into the snowy woods and…vanished.

Back down in the basement, Conrad and Pete lay unconscious in a fog of thick smoke laced with tear gas. When Andrew, who had been upstairs guarding the front lobby, decided to check on his two friends and found the basement filled with smoke, he immediately jumped into action. He located Pete's body, dragged the man into the elevator, and then went back for Conrad.

"What in the world…" Andrew muttered, dragging Conrad's body into the old, creepy elevator, feeling his back crying out in pain. "Hold on, guys…" Andrew hit a silver button that sent the old elevator creeping up to the first floor. "Andy…go get Doc Downing…two men are down…go!" he yelled at a thin broomstick of a man who was standing guard in the front lobby. Andy spotted Conrad and Pete lying unconscious in the elevator and took off like a scalded cat. Andrew took in a deep breath, bent down, and began checking his friends for any signs of life. "Breathing…alive. Thank you, Lord!"

An hour later, Conrad rubbed his forehead, felt a white bandage, and mumbled something to himself. "I'm gonna clobber Alvin the Great if it's the last thing I do!" he promised and then walked his eyes around the stuffy brown and blue examining room. Pete was sitting in the corner of the room in a brown chair also rubbing his forehead. "You okay?"

Pete held up his hand. "I'll live," he said in a grumpy voice, feeling like a cop who had been knocked silly with a wet bag of sand. "We let the body…" Pete closed his eyes. "Is this Alaska or Los Angeles?"

"Alaska," Andrew told Pete, leaning against the examining room door. The man hated hospitals. The sight of blood pressure machines, heart monitors, needles—it all gave Andrew the creeps. "Well, at least we know that Alvin the Great is behind this."

Pete opened his eyes. "I'm not so sure," he stated.

"What do you mean?" Andrew asked, frowning, tired and ready for a warm bed and a hot bowl of tomato soup along with a peanut butter and jelly sandwich. "Who else could it have been, Pete?"

Conrad studied Pete's face. "What're your thoughts, Pete?"

"The voice that I heard before my lights went out…the voice sounded like it belonged to a man who had to be at least forty-five or older. Raymond A. Mayfield is thirty-five. But," Pete carefully added, "that's not what caught my attention." Pete rubbed his forehead. "Right before my lights went out, I heard the door to the morgue open."

"I was standing right at the door, Pete," Conrad pointed out. Pete gave Conrad a *think real hard* look. Conrad let his shoulders slump. "Well, when the smoke exploded, I might have moved two or three feet away from the door—but not far enough away for a person to slip past me."

"Alvin the Great is a magician," Pete pointed out. "Guys, I'm thinking that Alvin the Great, a.k.a. Raymond A. Mayfield, stole the body of Senator Mayfield before someone else could."

Before Conrad could respond, Sarah knocked on the examining room door. Andrew quickly move out of the way, opened the door, and let in a very worried, cold pregnant woman drenched with snow.

"Sarah, what in the world?" Conrad exclaimed, jumping to his feet and running to Sarah, ignoring the slight dizziness he felt. "I told you to stay home!"

Sarah wrapped her arms around Conrad. "Manford used his skis to go get Amanda's snowmobile. Amanda then drove me to the hospital," she explained. "Oh, are you okay?"

"I'm okay," Conrad promised. He began brushing snow off Sarah's white coat and then gently removed the pink muffler she was wearing and kissed her cold nose. "You shouldn't have come."

Amanda stepped into the crowded room and yanked off her blue hat with shaky hands. "I've…never been so cold in all of my life," she stated through shivering teeth. "I'll never feel warm again as long as I live."

Pete looked at poor Amanda and then watched the frozen woman begin peeling ice off her eyebrows. "Is it cold outside?" he tried to joke and then winced as a sharp pain grabbed his head. "I guess I deserved that."

Sarah walked over to Pete and studied the bandage on his forehead. "Are you okay, partner?" she asked.

Pete pointed at Sarah's belly. "I'm fine. It was foolish to come out in this storm."

"When Andrew called me…what choice was there?" Sarah asked, turning back to Conrad and taking his hand. "Alvin called me right before I left the cabin. He wanted me to inform the cops that he wasn't the one who attacked you."

"Sarah—" Conrad began.

Sarah held up her hand. "Alvin did claim he has the body of Senator Mayfield, but," she added, "he's not going to turn it over until we catch the killer. Oh, and he's not happy that we, in his own words, disrupted his 'lodging environment' but blames himself for not outsmarting the cops."

"Great," Conrad fussed. "We have a real loon on our hands running around in a snowstorm with a stolen body."

"That's right, you bloke," Amanda fired at Conrad and then kicked his leg. "Get out there and catch the real killer before Alvin the Great drives us all mad!"

Conrad let out a yell, grabbed his leg, and backed away from Amanda. "That's it," he growled and began going for his handcuffs. Pete quickly grabbed his arm. "Oh, come on, Pete. I've been wanting to arrest this woman for years."

"You just try!" Amanda dropped down into a silly fighting position and began bouncing around. "Come on...I'll smear you!"

Sarah rolled her eyes. Yes, she was grateful Conrad and Pete were both alive and well, but good grief, now wasn't the time to see her husband and best friend have a boxing match. However, the sight of Pete holding Conrad's arm back and Amanda bouncing around like a silly cat was pretty funny.

"Give me strength," Sarah begged.

"I'll smear the floor with you...you bloke!"

"Pete...just let me get my handcuffs!" Conrad yelled.

Outside, the snowstorm raged on while Tom Jamison slithered back to a hidden cabin and Alvin the Great broke into Sarah's coffee shop with a dead body.

Yes, murder and mystery in a snowstorm, Sarah thought—along with a furious husband and angry best friend—made life very interesting.

"Handcuffs, Pete—now!"

"I'll smear you!"

5

Alvin stored Senator Mayfield's body in the small office resting in the back kitchen of Sarah's coffee shop, turned off the heat, and hauled butt out the back door. Because the power was out and the coffee shop was operating off generator power, entry and escape was fairly simple. Also, the security alarm, which any bozo could bypass, wasn't very difficult to outsmart. For now, Alvin assumed, stepping out into a frozen, white, snow-filled alley full of howling winds, the body of Senator Mayfield was safe; or so he hoped.

"Alvin the Great must roam the frozen tundra and keep watch for the enemy," he whispered in a brave stage voice that even to himself sounded dorky and lame. He quickly slammed a black ski mask over his face, yanked a black hood over his head, tucked his body into the icy winds, and began walking down the alley. Five minutes later, he turned around and hurried back to the coffee shop. "Too cold...Alvin the Great needs to warm up first," he said through shivering teeth as he stepped back into the kitchen of the coffee shop, closed the door, and quickly turned the heat back up.

As Alvin warmed his hands, Sarah stood studying the small black box that had begun beeping in her purse. "Someone tripped the hidden laser at the coffee shop," she explained. "Three guesses who."

Conrad rubbed the back of his neck. "I think we know who the winner is."

"It's a good thing you had those lasers installed," Andrew said as he checked his gun. "Using a dummy security system was also smart."

"A trick Pete taught me," Sarah explained, smiling at Pete as she put the black box away. "Well, I guess we better get moving."

"We?" Conrad scoffed. "No, ma'am. Amanda is taking you right back to the cabin."

Sarah shook her head. "Conrad, the hospital is seven good miles from our home and less than a mile from town. I'm not up for another seven-mile ride, not in this weather."

"Me, neither," Amanda said. "What are you…fruity in the head?" She rolled her eyes and then grabbed Sarah's hand. "Come on, love, I'll drive you to the coffee shop. Maybe we'll finally catch Alvin the Great."

"My wife will ride with me," Conrad informed Amanda. "Pete, you drive that loudmouth back to town, okay?"

"Loudmouth…why, I should flatten your lip!" Amanda shook her fists at Conrad. Conrad rolled his eyes. "One day, you bloke…your body will vanish and be buried deep in the Alaskan wilderness."

"You two," Sarah sighed, having had enough. "Conrad… Amanda…you know what, you two drive back to town together. Pete, you're with me. Let's go." Sarah grabbed Pete's hand and walked him out of the hospital, leaving Conrad and Amanda fussing at each other as they followed.

"See what you did? You upset my wife!" Conrad barked at Amanda, slapping on a pair of black winter gloves.

"I did no such thing…idiot," Amanda barked back as she slapped on her muffler and prepared for an icy ride. She glanced behind her and saw Andrew grinning. "Don't make me slug you!"

Andrew threw up his hands. "No, ma'am…"

Sarah giggled to herself as she walked out into the snowstorm with Pete and made her way to a green snowmobile parked out front. "Those two," she told Pete.

Pete shoved a cigar into his mouth, climbed onto the snowmobile, and patted the back seat. "Hop on, kiddo, Old Pete is ready to ride."

Sarah carefully made her way onto the snowmobile, with Pete's help, of course, and put on a green helmet. Pete slapped on a gray helmet, brought the snowmobile to life, and got moving. "Hold on!" he called out.

"I'm holding…I'm holding!" Sarah called back, holding onto Pete as tightly as possible, feeling as if the snowmobile helmet she was wearing was going to squeeze her head in half. "I thought being pregnant was supposed to be fun!" she called out as Pete took the snowmobile out onto the street and aimed the nose toward town. Of course, any sane eye couldn't tell that there was a street running in front of the hospital—and honestly, Pete just hoped he was on the street. If not, he figured Sarah would probably tell him he was going the wrong way. Snow always transformed the world into a mysterious atmosphere that turned a simple street into a white trail of danger and confusion.

"You just hold on!" Pete yelled, keeping the snowmobile at a steady speed as the snow and winds attacked his body, eating through his thick overcoat and grabbing at his skin. Pete reckoned he had never felt such cold before—a cold he was going to have to become friends with.

"Hurry up," Amanda complained to Conrad back in the hospital parking lot. "I can barely see them!"

Conrad jumped onto Amanda's blue snowmobile, snatched on a gray helmet, waited for Amanda to get situated, and then hit the gas. "Hold on!"

Amanda nearly lost her balance and tumbled off the back of the snowmobile. She let out a cry, grabbed Conrad's shoulder, and yelled, "You crazy bloke…I'm going to murder you!" Conrad grinned. It was fun having a woman who had become a sister fussing up a storm. Why? Because he was the one driving the snowmobile and there was absolutely nothing Amanda could do. "I'm going to—"

"Hold on!" Conrad yelled and ordered the snowmobile to pick up speed, sliding out onto the road at a dangerous angle and then racing to catch up to Sarah and Pete. Amanda nearly slipped off the back of the snowmobile again and then began trying to choke Conrad. Conrad grinned, tucked his head down, and raced up behind Sarah and Conrad.

Sarah turned her head, saw Amanda struggling to choke her husband, and giggled. "Those two!" she called out to Pete. Pete nodded his head and focused on making it to town without turning into a snowman. Sarah tucked her head down against the wind and held on.

By the time Pete parked a few stores down from the coffee shop, he felt frozen to the core but managed to climb off the snowmobile and take out his gun. "I'll…cover the alley," he said through chattering teeth.

Conrad jumped off Amanda's snowmobile, taking a few punches as he did, and jogged up to Pete. "I'll take the alley, Pete. You cover the front," he said as he yanked out his gun.

Pete hesitated and then nodded his head in agreement. In the old days, Pete always secured the alley; however, he was standing in a small northern Alaska town being beaten down by a fierce snowstorm searching for a crazed magician. The thought of forcing his frozen body through the snow and circling around back in order to secure a frozen wind tunnel didn't exactly sit well in his mind. "Take off."

Conrad gave Sarah a quick kiss on her frozen nose. "Give me ten minutes and then go into the coffee shop."

"Ten minutes." Sarah nodded her head and then gave Conrad a *be careful* look. "Please." Conrad smiled and ran off into the snowstorm with his gun at the ready just as Andrew appeared on a brown snowmobile. Sarah watched as Conrad stopped Andrew, talked for a few seconds, and then took off running again. Andrew quickly jumped off the snowmobile and followed. "Two is better than one," Sarah whispered, grateful that a good, decent man like Andrew had joined her husband.

"Love," Amanda complained, tucking her head down against the icy winds and hugging her arms, "why did you marry that bloke?"

"Love." Sarah smiled. She took Amanda's hand and carefully began walking her toward the coffee shop. The howling winds, she knew, were disguising every exterior sound, including the sound of the snowmobiles. Sarah had spent many winter nights inside her coffee shop listening to the winds while trucks and snowmobiles crawled up and down the street. The only sounds that floated into Sarah's ears now were the sounds of angry, lonely, crying, howling winds.

"Remind me to have you admitted to a mental home after your twins are born," Amanda warned and then touched Sarah's tender tummy. "How are you feeling, by the way?"

Sarah stopped walking. "Cold and tired," she admitted, "but I'm not ready for the drive back to the cabin." Sarah studied the storm-battered main street, looked at snow-soaked shops that she knew by heart, and then let her eyes rest on a street that was knee deep in snow. "It's amazing how snow changes the world, isn't it?" she asked as her teeth began to chatter.

"We can talk inside," Pete begged, hugging his arms, struggling to keep warm.

Sarah managed to ignore the cold in her mind as her eyes studied the snow with…love. "The snow hides me away," she whispered and then started moving. By the time she reached the front door of the coffee shop, ten minutes had nearly passed. "Okay…let's get inside," she said, digging a set of keys out of her purse and then pulling out a gun. "June Bug, unlock the front door. Pete and I will cover you."

Amanda took the keys with shaky hands covered by thick winter gloves that felt useless against the cold, looked at Sarah with a careful eye, and then carefully began unlocking the front door.

Alvin, who was sitting in the kitchen at a small, round, wooden table, had no idea that Conrad and Andrew were in the back alley. In Alvin's mind, he was safely hidden in a very clever location. Yes, he was a clever, brave hero who had turned a simple coffee shop into a hidden cave—a hero who had outsmarted a simple security system and was now warming his frozen body; a hero who had no clue that he had set off a hidden alarm.

"Alvin the Great will warm himself and then…" Alvin said, talking to himself, pretending to be a great hero, but stopped when he heard the front door of the coffee shop open. The poor guy nearly wet his pants. "Oh crud!" Alvin fell back in his chair, scrambled to his feet, and took off for the back door. But as soon as he yanked open the back door, he saw Conrad shove a gun at him. "Oh crud!" Alvin slammed the door shut with panicked hands, studied the kitchen, and then reached into his coat pocket and yanked out a few smoke bombs. "Alvin the Great…mustn't be caught," he said in a panicked voice. He activated the smoke bombs and then yanked open the back door just as Pete charged into the kitchen.

Conrad saw the back door burst open again. White, heavy smoke immediately began flooding out into the alley. "Not this time, pal!" he yelled, slapping smoke from his face and stepping into the doorway with his gun at the ready. "You're not escaping! Andrew…cover my back!" Andrew slapped smoke away from his own face and began moving his gun around, searching for any signs of human movement.

Pete, hearing Conrad yell at Andrew to cover his back, moved through the thick smoke toward the back door. "Conrad…moving toward you!" he yelled.

"I've got the kitchen entrance secured!" Sarah called out, standing in the doorway leading into the front room with her gun at the ready.

"We've got you this time, pal!" Conrad hollered, moving into the kitchen with Andrew covering his back. "You've got nowhere to run…give yourself up!"

Pete spotted Conrad's body in the smoke and then looked to his left and right. That's when the reality of the situation struck him like a sour cheeseburger hitting the belly of a hungry alley cat. "Ah…he got away!" Pete roared and kicked the floor.

"What? Impossible…he's in the kitchen somewhere!" Conrad demanded, meeting up with Pete as the white smoke began to thin out.

"But where?" Pete asked, stepping out into the alley. The alley, although filled with white smoke, was…clear. "Magicians…they all need to be shot," he fussed and hurried back into the kitchen, leaving Andrew to stand watch at the kitchen door.

"How?" Conrad cried in a desperate voice. He threw his hands up into the air and marched off to the small office. "We've got the body…at least we have that!"

Sarah joined Conrad, spotted Senator Mayfield slumped over at an old, worn-down wooden desk, and sighed. "We're never going to catch Alvin the Great," she told Conrad, patting her husband's shoulder before leaving the kitchen. "June Bug, make me a pot of coffee, please…I need to rest."

"Sure thing, love," Amanda promised and ordered Andrew to close the blimey back door before she froze to death. Andrew jumped out of his skin, closed the back door, and joined Conrad and Pete at the office door. Amanda rolled her eyes and set out to make a couple of pots of hot coffee.

Sarah sat down at a cozy table and plopped her chin down onto her gloved hands. As she did, her eyes spotted movement at the front door. "Huh?" she asked, raising her head. She spotted Alvin yank open the front door with a smile, wave at her, and then vanish into the snow. "But… how…I mean…" Sarah raised her hands in frustration and then dropped them. "No sense in trying to chase him down…"

Alvin, who had barely managed to escape the clutches of people he considered "reluctant allies," ran off into the snow with a racing heart, realizing that he had barely escaped being captured. Sure, he had given Sarah a theatrical smile before departing the coffee shop—but deep down he was shaking all over. Being a hero wasn't as easy as the dopes in the movies made it out to be. In real life, being a hero took real brains and real courage—something a bunch of sissy, pampered actors didn't have. "Alvin the Great will not be defeated," Alvin promised as he escaped into the woods resting behind the frozen alley. "Alvin the Great will win this battle…and regain his career…while making sure his enemies perish!"

While Alvin ran off into the snow, Sarah sat rubbing her eyes, wondering how in the world Raymond A. Mayfield had managed to escape from the coffee shop. It was obvious the guy was a pretty tricky magician, which made Sarah wonder if she should entertain the idea of learning a few magic tricks herself in order to catch Alvin the Great at his own game. "Maybe." Sarah sighed and waited for Amanda to bring her a hot cup of coffee. It was going to be a long, snowy, cold day and Little Sarah and Little Conrad were not the least bit happy. No sir. The two beautiful twin babies resting safely in their mother's womb were discussing the idea of seeing what all the fuss was about in the outside world.

"Okay, so we have the body...let's keep the body this time," Pete growled. "And while we're at it, we better turn down this heat or this body is going to start getting pretty ripe."

Andrew rubbed the back of his neck. "I'll have Andy and Steve take the body back to the hospital," he said. He walked to the back door, opened it, and ordered the two frozen men to step inside. "You guys take the body back to the hospital and guard it," he explained in a concerned voice. "Andy, you stand inside the morgue next to the body, and Steve, you stay in the office. I'll have Michael guard the hallway."

Andy frowned. Making a trip back to the hospital was like having someone rip his eyebrows out. "Do we have to?"

"I'm afraid so," Andrew told Andy, patting the man's thin shoulder and then looking at Steve. Steve was the opposite of Pete. The man, although not entirely fat, was built like a chubby grizzly bear. "We're working overtime, guys. Sorry."

"Part of the job, right?" Steve said, slapping snow off the brown coat he was wearing and nodding at Conrad. "Don't worry, we'll guard the body…unlike those two city cops," he teased.

"Yeah," Andy jumped in. "City cops aren't fit for small-town action, right, Steve?" He nudged Steve with his elbow and then grinned at Conrad. Roasting Conrad was fun. "Don't worry, Detective, we'll make sure the stiff stays put this time."

"All right, you guys," Andrew warned.

Andy and Steve laughed. "Oh, Conrad knows we're only teasing. Besides, we're in no hurry to get back out into the storm."

Pete leaned against the kitchen counter studying Andy and Steve, deciding whether he wanted to shoot the two clowns or wait until later when no witnesses were present. "Get the body back to the hospital before it turns ripe," he ordered, shoving a cigar into his mouth and narrowing his eyes. "This city cop isn't in the mood to be roasted, boys."

Andy and Steve read Pete's eyes. Andy shot Steve a worried glance. "Uh…yeah, sure," he told Pete. Pete simply nodded his head while patting the gun that was hidden under his overcoat.

"Those two are good cops, Pete," Andrew stepped in, hoping to prevent bloodshed—or at least prevent Pete from kicking Andy's and Steve's butts up and down the frozen alley. Pete, Andrew knew, was not a man to be pushed around. "All right you guys, enough kidding. Get the body back to the hospital."

Conrad walked over to the back door, opened it, studied the stormy alley, and then looked back at Pete and Andrew. "Storm is getting worse. I don't think Pete and Steve need to leave town. Maybe they should put the body in the basement of the station. The basement is almost as cold as it is outside. It's like an iceberg down in that hole."

Andrew considered Conrad's suggestion. "Yeah, okay," he agreed. "We might have a better chance of guarding the body at the station anyway. There's only one door leading in and out of the basement."

"Well, there are the three basement windows," Andy pointed out.

"Piled over with snow," Steve added and gave Andy a *boy, are you dumb* look. "You'd have to be a magician to get into the basement."

"Well, sparky, that's exactly what Alvin Mayfield is," Andy popped, slapping Steve's blue and white police muffler off and rolling his eyes.

"Hey…watch it!" Steve fussed as he tried to catch his hat.

"All right, you two, enough," Andrew ordered and then let out a tired laugh. "You two haven't changed since we were in school."

"Nope." Andy smiled, slapped Steve on his shoulder, and then eyed the door leading into the small office. "Steve and I have been friends since we were seven years old…not much has changed," he explained. "Well, we might as well get to work, huh?"

"Might as well," Steve said, picking up his hat and then walking into the small office with Andy. A few minutes later, he backed out carrying Senator Mayfield's legs while Andy worked on carrying the dead man's shoulders.

Andrew quickly opened the back door. "Better if Sarah doesn't see," he told his two friends. "With her being pregnant with the twins and all."

Pete checked his gun and then followed Andy and Steve out into the frozen alley. "I'll follow these two back to the station and make sure the body gets put in the basement," he told Conrad. "You stay with the two girls. Andrew… you better come with me."

"You got it, Pete." Andrew slapped on his muffler, pulled out his gun, and trailed after Pete.

"I'll be at the station within the hour," Conrad called out. He closed and locked the back door, reset the dummy alarm, and then carefully reset the laser alarm. "That should do it," he said in a confident voice, studying the warm kitchen before walking into the front room. "Andy and Steve are carrying the body back to the station. We're going to store the body in the station's basement," he explained. "Pete and Andrew are covering their rear."

Sarah nodded her head, took a sip of hot coffee, and studied the front door. "Alvin was wearing a black ski mask. I didn't see his face. I also didn't see how he managed to get into this room without being seen."

"Tell me about it," Conrad said, walking over to the front door and studying the lock. "This guy isn't a genius, but he's obviously not dumb."

"Unlike some I know," Amanda told Conrad in an accusing voice. "Boy, three cops and you let Alvin the Great escape. Talk about dumb...D.U.M.B." Amanda picked up a cinnamon roll, took a bite, and then continued. "I wouldn't be the least bit shocked if that dead bloke ended up missing again. Cops...yeesh."

"Hey, look, it isn't our fault—" Conrad began to tear into Amanda with sharp teeth.

Sarah quickly held up her hand. "Not now," she begged. "And June Bug...well...you do have a point."

"Thanks a lot," Conrad complained.

"No, what I mean," Sarah clarified, "is that we all seem to be defenseless against Alvin the Great's appearing and vanishing acts. And now we also have to worry about a second unknown person who seems to be using the same MO as Alvin the Great, and right now we have absolutely no clue as to who the guy is."

"Bunch of clowns," Amanda fussed. "Smoke… appearing…vanishing…stealing a dead body…sick!"

Sarah rubbed her chin. "Well, we do know that Raymond A. Mayfield did steal items from O'Mally's that are connected to magic shows. Smoke bombs…old fireworks…mirrors…things of that nature. It's my belief that Alvin the Great is going to attempt to become a superhero in order to restart his career as a magician." Sarah took a sip of coffee. "This morning when I woke up, I spent about half an hour doing some more research before cooking breakfast."

Conrad walked over to the table Sarah and Amanda were sitting at, looked down into the face of his beautiful wife, and nodded. "What did my little detective dig up?"

"Raymond A. Mayfield's career was starting to fail," Sarah explained. "His acts were becoming outdated. New and upcoming magicians were quickly pushing Rusty Smoke out into a cold alley. And it was about that time that the guy decided to return to Boise…later on, he announced that he was going to run for governor."

Conrad studied Sarah's eyes. "But?"

"I'm wondering if Senator Mayfield manipulated his son," Sarah said. She took some more coffee down and studied the interior of the coffee shop. The interior, which still resembled the 1930s, felt warm and inviting—felt like home. Sarah loved her coffee shop; adored it. Sure, the coffee shop was scarcely open for business, but Sarah knew that after the twins were born and when she had the time, she would open the coffee shop for at least three, maybe four days a week; or so she hoped. The coffee shop wasn't a money-making business by any means—and Sarah surely didn't need the money. No, the coffee shop was an old friend that needed to be visited every so often with a loving smile and warm hello.

But now wasn't the time to think about how many days Sarah might be able to keep the coffee shop open. "If I could just get Raymond A. Mayfield to sit down and talk to us."

"Fat chance, love," Amanda laughed, shoving more cinnamon roll into her mouth and tossing a thumb up at Conrad. "With that bloke on the job…along with the other stooges…we've got more of a chance of a hungry grizzly bear rolling over and letting us pet his tummy than catching Alvin the Great."

Conrad shot Amanda a sour eye. "Don't push it," he growled. "I don't see you coming up with any ideas…like the pea brain inside of your head could come up with any sensible ideas."

"Well, you smelly bloke," Amanda stated, washing down her bite of cinnamon roll with some hot coffee, "it just so happens that the little pea brain inside of my head has come up with a very clever idea."

"I don't think taking Alvin the Great shopping is a clever idea," Conrad groaned.

"Oh, shove a flat tire into that empty head of yours," Amanda told Conrad and then shook her fist at him. "I should flatten your lip…but…I'm a lady, so I will simply tell my dear, lovely friend my idea."

Sarah grinned. Amanda never failed to brighten her day. "Yes, June Bug, what is your idea?"

"A net."

"A net?" Conrad asked. "Are you kidding me? That's the dumbest plan—"

"Please," Sarah begged, patting Amanda's hand and nodding at her best friend to continue.

"Thank you, love," Amanda said. She raised her chin, huffed, and then proudly continued to explain her clever idea. "We currently have Senator Mayfield back in our possession, which means that eventually two things are going to occur. One," Amanda held up one finger, "Alvin the Great is going to come for the body, and two," Amanda held up two fingers, "the bloke who put your lights out is going to come for the body—which means we now have the opportunity to catch two birds with one…net."

Conrad hated to admit it, but Amanda's plan did have appeal. "The body is being put in a cold, icy basement as we speak. The basement has one door…and three windows. The snow has the windows buried under and they're most likely frozen closed anyway, which means that the basement door will be the only entry and exit point."

Amanda shook her head. "You need to take the body back to the hospital. We have to give Alvin the Great room to breathe. Besides, the second, unseen bloke probably won't attempt to steal a dead body from a police station."

"I'm not so certain," Conrad objected. "It seems to me that Mona Jamison is desperate to make sure no official autopsy is conducted on Senator Mayfield. Desperate people do—"

"Desperate things…yeah, yeah, I know." Amanda rolled her eyes. "I've watched enough black-and-white detective movies to know the scene. Besides, I'm not a rookie anymore. This little English Muffin has fought her share of bad guys, too, you know."

"Yes, you have," Sarah told Amanda, patting her best friend's hand. She looked up at Conrad. "Amanda has saved my life…and your life, Conrad. She's been standing at my side from the very first day I moved to Snow Falls, and she's almost been killed—numerous times—because of her faithfulness to our friendship. She deserves to be treated with respect, okay?"

Conrad thought back to the time when a crazed model had targeted Sarah in Snow Falls, building snowmen wearing leather jackets before finally deciding to carry out a murderous attack. Amanda had saved the day…saving not only Sarah's life but his life as well. "Yeah, you saved our backsides more than once."

"In Oregon, that insane teenager had the upper hand on me and was about to fill me full of bullets. If Amanda hadn't shown up when she did and slugged him in the face, I wouldn't be sitting here," Sarah told Conrad.

"Well…all in a day's work, love." Amanda blushed. "I mean, it's nothing…really."

"You shot the Back Alley Killer," Sarah pointed out. "You saved our lives."

"Well…that creep's daughter nearly cut my head off with a kitchen knife," Amanda told Sarah. "Talk about seeing my life flash before my eyes. Let me tell you, being tied down to a kitchen chair while running from a killer trying to chop you to pieces with a kitchen knife isn't fun."

Sarah patted Amanda's hand again. "June Bug, you are and will forever be my hero," she promised and then looked up at Conrad. "I think we should listen to Amanda and follow her plan."

Conrad rubbed his chin. "What do we have to lose?" he asked.

"A dead body," Amanda quipped and then shrugged her shoulders. "But it wouldn't be the first time," she teased and grinned at Conrad. "Right?"

Conrad rolled his eyes. "Knock it off, okay?"

"Three cops…shame, shame, shame." Amanda kept up her attack, determined to pay Conrad back for nearly scaring the life out of her while driving to town on her snowmobile. "Three cops…and in a snowstorm, too. My goodness…is that the way you Yanks operate in New York? No wonder that sewer hole is so full of rats."

"Hey…New York may be polluted with corruption, but it's still a good place. Kinda. Well, it was in the older days… kinda." Conrad winced. "Way back when…"

"Corrupt politicians and goofy mafia clowns…sounds like my type of town." Amanda grinned. "And don't forget that one of those goofy mafia clowns followed you all the way to Alaska."

Conrad winced again. "Yeah…"

Sarah smiled. "Oh, don't be so hard on yourself. So what if you, Pete, and Andrew let Alvin the Great escape. It… happens." Sarah tucked her head down and giggled. Conrad blushed and then hurried off to the bathroom, unable to take the heat anymore. "Well, June Bug," Sarah laughed, watching her husband escape, "now what?"

"Now we wait until night falls and then get that body back to the hospital. And then we wait," Amanda explained, grabbing another cinnamon roll. She studied Sarah's eyes. "In the meantime, why don't you tell me what your brain has been thinking, because I know you're up to something."

Sarah nodded. Yes, the pregnant, beautiful detective was indeed up to something.

6

"He stole the body!" Tom Jamison yelled into a brown telephone as he yanked a snow-soaked ski mask off his head, revealing the face of a forty-five-year-old man with dark gray hair that was supposed to radiate brilliance but instead cast arrogance over a hard, mean face.

Mona Jamison, who was standing in a luxury hotel room in Anchorage, felt her cheeks turn red. She threw her cold, deadly eyes at Ryan Elderson and then marched over to a window, yanked back a set of silk green curtains, and looked out at a city that was being battered by a vicious snowstorm. "I can't trust you to do anything!"

Ryan Elderson, a spineless worm who took orders from Mona Jamison, pretended to straighten the blue tie attached to the gray suit he was wearing and then proceeded to make sure his gray hair was in order before leaving the hotel room to visit the restaurant downstairs and get a bite to eat. Mona threw him a *don't you dare* eye.

Ryan froze. In the eyes of the world, the man was a cruel politician bent on destroying the moral foundation America was built on—but behind closed doors he was a spineless coward who took orders from people like Mona Jamison and other people who filled his pockets full of money. Ryan Elderson was a face and nothing more—a face hired by deadly people to appease a decaying public.

Senator Mayfield had been a face, too…but the foolish man had decided to break the rules and override the power Mona was controlling him with—the foolish man had even decided to bring his son into the picture, manipulate the poor lad, and have him take the fall for murdering Mona Jamison. Of course, Mona had become wise to the plan and set out to kill her husband…well, political husband. However, now it seemed that, even though Mona had succeeded in killing Senator Mayfield, she was in a dangerous bind. If an autopsy was conducted on Senator Mayfield, the findings would certainly be damaging.

"I'm hungry, Mona. And it seems that you and your son have much to talk about."

Tom stomped snow off the black boots he was wearing and threw his angry eyes around a warm kitchen that to any decent soul would appear inviting and cozy, especially with a snowstorm blazing outside. Tom Jamison was far from decent and in a very dangerous situation. If an autopsy was carried out on Senator Mayfield, a lot of powerful people were going to take a deadly fall—people who would most certainly ensure that Tom ended up dead before they were shipped off to prison.

But what worried Tom the most was his own mother. Yes, Mona Jamison would be the person planning his murder. "Send Ryan out of the room. We don't need him."

Mona narrowed her eyes and then pointed at the hotel room door. "Bring me back a tuna salad sandwich, a salad, an orange juice, and some fruit." Ryan, acting like a beaten down dog who had been given a few minutes to heal, nodded his head and scurried away, tossing a wary eye at the woman with short gray hair and a face filled with a mean, cold, soulless cruelty. "You must locate Raymond and kill him," she hissed at Tom and quickly brushed at the dark gray dress she was wearing, hoping to appear stylish rather than old and dried up.

Tom knew Alvin despised his first name and insisted people refer to him using his middle name. Mona had never honored Alvin's wishes. "How?" he asked in a furious voice. "The storm that has crippled the state is growing stronger by the minute. I have no idea where Alvin—"

"Raymond."

"Who cares?" Tom snapped. "I have no idea where the rat is hiding and where he stashed the body." Tom sat down at a square, polished kitchen table holding a bowl of plastic fruit, ignoring the strain he was putting on the telephone cord. "If the authorities perform an autopsy, they'll find the drug I put in Mayfield's drink. The plan was to give the man a heart attack and have our own people carry out the autopsy."

"Yes, yes," Mona complained, "I'm fully aware of the plan. I'm also fully aware our target escaped to Alaska before you could stop him."

Tom gritted his teeth. "The pill is designed to kill the intended victim when alcohol is introduced into the blood stream. We all know Mayfield was a drunk…but I couldn't get him to drink a drop. I was forced to place the pill into a glass of milk, hoping that sooner or later he would go for a bottle of the rum he liked. When I left his home—"

"You left the house assuming the man was still under my control," Mona snapped. "As soon as you left, he escaped and flew to Alaska."

"Okay…okay…so Mayfield pulled the rug over my eyes," Tom fired back. "I'm here now, aren't I? I'm doing all of the dirty work."

Mona rubbed her eyes. Her son was not only bothersome, weak, whiny, and problematic, he was arrogant and self-centered and consumed with excuses that supported his self-pitying attitude. "Mayfield got you drunk while he remained sober…it's your fault he escaped. Which means it's your responsibility to clean up the mess."

"Hey, I managed to sneak the pill into Mayfield's milk…" Tom gritted his teeth again. Oh, how he despised his mother. However, the woman kept him working as a crummy city attorney (in order to carry out her criminal work, of course) and his pocket full of money. The woman also had a lot of dirt on him that a jury would devour with greedy hands. "Look…I admit that I let Mayfield slip past me, okay?"

"All you had to do was make the man drink a little rum while I was out of town!" Mona screamed. "The plan was perfect!"

Tom knew Mona had stepped out onto a red hot field consumed with fury and rage. The woman, he feared, was most likely going to have him killed even if he did manage to locate Senator Mayfield's body and kill Alvin. Of course, Tom had believed his mother had planned his murder more than once in the past and here he was, still alive—so maybe, if he managed to clean up the mess he created, Mona might allow him to live. One thing was for certain—he was losing the battle of tempers. "No one is going anywhere in this storm…Alvin has to be staying somewhere. I need you to start checking all the rental cabins."

Mona could have burst into a ball of flames. "Don't tell me what to do!"

"You want the body, don't you?" Tom asked. "We need to work as a team."

"This coming from a drunk who can't even defend a pickpocket!" Mona slammed the curtains closed, stormed over to the writing desk, nearly yanking the phone cord out of the wall, sat down, and snatched up a pen.

"Ryan is having second thoughts," she informed Tom, temporarily changing direction. "I can read his eyes." Mona began doodling on a white piece of paper. She always doodled when her temper was flaring. Why? She didn't know. An old elementary school habit, she guessed. "We have to kill him."

Tom closed his eyes. Killing Ryan Elderson was out of the question. "We need to focus on Mayfield first and get ourselves in the clear."

"Ryan knows we killed Mayfield, you idiot!" Mona pressed the pen she was holding down so hard she broke through the paper she was doodling on. "Of course, that's another one of your…mistakes, which means you must kill the man…or else."

Tom swallowed. "I…understand," he assured Mona, feeling his own anger and rage dripping out of his chest and landing on the polished hardwood floor. Mona's tone clearly told Tom that his fear of being murdered was soon going to become a reality if he didn't obey. "I'll…let me handle Mayfield and his son…and then we'll focus on Elderson."

"I'll have the rental cabins checked," Mona told Tom, returning to the issue at hand, pleased that she had caged in her weak and spineless son. Motherhood, at least to Mona Jamison, was such a bothersome chore. "In the meantime, stay at the cabin you're in and wait for my call. No…on the other hand, go back to the hospital and stay out of sight."

"Easier said than done. The hospital here is small and—"

"Remain outside in the snow!" Mona yelled.

"I'll freeze!"

"Then freeze!" Mona yelled again, throwing down her pen and standing up. So much for doodling. "The police may locate Alvin and retrieve the body…which means you must watch the hospital!"

Tom had no intention of venturing back out into the storm. "Yes, all right," he lied, fully intending to stay indoors. Besides, there was no way Mona would—or could—ever know the truth. Staying indoors next to a warm fire was far more important at the moment than watching a small hospital in an icy snowstorm, freezing to death. And it wasn't likely the police were going to locate Alvin or the missing body anyway.

"I will call you first thing tomorrow morning. In the meantime, keep watch and call me if anything important develops."

"I will," Tom assured Mona and then asked, "What if… Alvin escapes with the body?"

"You die," Mona hissed and ended the call, leaving Tom sitting in a state of fear.

Tom stood up, put the telephone away with shaky hands, and then decided to make a pot of coffee. "She's going to kill me," he worried. "Even if I kill Alvin and find the body…it's foolish to think she won't kill me. Maybe in the past my life was spared…but not this time."

Deep down Tom knew that Mona Jamison was going to hire someone to murder him. He began pacing around the polished kitchen, desperately trying to think. After about half an hour of pacing back and forth, an idea struck his arrogant mind. "I have no choice but to run. I have money stored up in an offshore account…yes…I have to run or my mother will have me killed."

With those words, Tom hurried to the telephone and called the Anchorage Airport and booked a flight to New Zealand. "As soon as the storm ends, I'm out of here. The show is all yours, Alvin," he said and began to make his way down the hallway that led to the master bedroom but not before throwing a pot pie into the oven of the stainless steel stove. He was hungry and needed food.

As Tom hurried down the hallway, something strange happened. A sharp pain struck Tom in his chest; a deep, paralyzing pain that brought Tom down to his knees.

"No…this can't…be happening," Tom managed to cry as death reached out and touched his heart. The last thing Tom Jamison remembered before dying was thinking, *Mayfield…got even with me…what's good for the goose… good for the gander…better than dying at the hands of that woman…*

Neither Sarah nor Alvin knew that Tom Jamison had died of a sudden, massive heart attack brought on by extreme stress, years of heavy drinking, years of eating greasy foods—and a vicious snowstorm that no man who was out of shape had any business roaming about in. No, Sarah was still sitting inside of her coffee shop assuming that a deadly, unknown figure was loose in Snow Falls, along with Alvin the Great.

Alvin, who was hunkered down in a gingerbread-style cottage that had been deserted for the winter—a cottage that belonged to Mrs. Bertha Madien, who flew to Arizona each winter to visit her daughter and grandchildren—was also under the assumption that Tom Jamison was still alive and active. Had Alvin known the man was dead, he would have simply put his plans on ice. After all, Alvin's plan was to capture Tom Jamison and make the man confess to his dark deeds in order to incriminate Mona Jamison. But irony always had a double-sided face that held humor and horror, and Sarah and Alvin were both trapped in the middle.

"Well, I guess we should…waddle on down to the station," Sarah sighed. "If I eat another cinnamon roll, I'm going to turn into a sugar cane."

Amanda quickly gobbled down one last cinnamon roll—her tenth—gulped down the last of her coffee, and stood up. "Love, are you certain?" she asked.

"I believe so," Sarah said, nodding. "All we can do is wait and see if my plan will work." Sarah held out her right hand. "Help me stand up, June Bug…my twin babies make it difficult." Amanda carefully helped Sarah stand up. Sarah smiled, gently touched her tummy, and whispered: "Mommy isn't complaining…mommy loves you both very, very much…with all of her heart."

"And so do I," Amanda promised. "Just do me a favor… don't pee on me, Little Conrad, like my son used to do, when I'm changing your diaper."

121

Sarah winced. "Pee?"

Amanda grinned. "My son used to pee straight up at his mum right when I opened his diaper." Amanda patted Sarah's arm. "You learn to have quick reflexes, love…and a careful eye."

"I…hope so." Sarah winced again, patted her tummy, and then walked over to the front door. "Well, if I get hit with a stream of pee…that's what being a mother is all about, right?"

"You bet." Amanda shoved on a pair of gloves and began working on a muffler and a scarf. "Diaper duty is the easy part, love…for a while. It's when the poopy begins to have a smell…not good."

Sarah slung a pink wool scarf around her neck. "You mean the…poop…doesn't smell at first?"

Amanda shook her head. "Not at first, love. But that's not the worst part…wait until your twins leave the bottle and start eating solids. Prepare for a nightmare."

"A nightmare?" Sarah gulped.

"Food all over you, your clothes, the floor, the walls… everywhere," Amanda explained. "And the poopy smell afterward…but that's all part of motherhood, love." Amanda winked at Sarah. "Don't worry, we'll make Manford feed the twins and Conrad change the diapers."

"If only," Sarah replied and then took a moment to ingest the images Amanda had thrown into her mind. "I look

THE MORE YOU SNOW

forward to changing every diaper and wiping up every bit of spilled food, June Bug."

"You know, love," Amanda said, smiling, "I did, too." Amanda took Sarah's gloved hand. "Motherhood is serious business and requires love and patience…but the memories…oh, the sweet memories…make every diaper and dish of spilled baby food worth it. Of course," Amanda teased as she unlocked and pulled open the front door, "just wait until your children become teenagers and start wanting to drive."

"Huh?" Sarah gasped as Amanda escaped out into the storm with a huge grin on her face. "Drive…oh boy…give me strength," Sarah whispered, touching her tummy. She drew in a deep breath and stepped out into the snow with the image of two wild and insane teenagers speeding around Snow Falls in a muscle car, terrorizing the public with Conrad blazing behind them in a police car screaming: "Now you kids cut that out!"

Oh, the joy of motherhood.

Night arrived. The snowstorm had turned into a growling creature ready to devour everything in its path. The town of Snow Falls was completely shut down. Nothing was moving, and every single citizen was hunkered down in their homes—well, every citizen except for a daring handful.

"Is Sarah still napping?" Conrad asked Pete.

Pete nodded. "Out like a light in one of the holding cells," he confirmed. He took a few seconds to chew on his cigar and then sat down behind Conrad's office desk. "Let the poor kid rest. We're not going anywhere."

"We need to get the body back to the hospital."

"Not in this weather." Pete shook his head. "I know Amanda's plan has merit, but it would be foolish to go out into this storm. The temperatures have dropped to a very dangerous level, Conrad." Pete shook his head again. "No, it's best if we sit tight for tonight right where we are."

"I agree," Andrew said, leaning in the office doorway holding a cup of coffee. "Senator Mayfield's body isn't going anywhere, and if we need another day to catch the bad guys, so be it."

Conrad shrugged his shoulders, looked out the office window at the dark, raging storm, and then let his shoulders drop. "You guys ever feel helpless?" he asked in a low voice.

"All the time," Pete confessed.

Conrad turned away from the office window. "I feel helpless to protect Sarah against the outside world... against all the monsters out there. Even in a little town like this, monsters seem to find their way in. And...now that the twins are due to arrive at any minute, it's a scary feeling knowing that you're not invincible. It's bad enough fighting the monsters posing as politicians...a world determined to protect evil and destroy good..."

"I know what you mean," Andrew told Conrad, sipping his coffee and taking a minute to listen to the screaming winds. "When my son was born, I wasn't certain what type of world he was going to grow up in. I vowed to keep him right here in Snow Falls, raise him up in the Bible, and pray that when he turned eighteen, he would have enough understanding to make all the right decisions." Andrew glanced down at his coffee cup. "The outside world is a scary place…full of killers, criminals…corrupt politicians…immorality…every darkness that a decent man stands against."

Andrew's words made images of Los Angeles—old and new—flood into Pete's mind. "The world is growing more evil by the day," Pete stated as he removed the cigar from his mouth. "Truth of the matter is, guys, I decided to leave L.A. because I knew the city had become a sinking ship that couldn't be saved. Many years ago, I once believed there was the possibility—however slim—that Los Angeles could still be saved. Now I know…the city is cursed and doomed to die a miserable death. Why? Because the hearts of those living in the city have rejected Jesus." Pete sighed. "Now, I'm not a perfect Christian by any means, and I'm sure not preaching, but Old Pete knows what happens to a country that rejects God."

"Snow Falls is still a Christian community," Andrew pointed out in a relieved voice. "We have our handful of hard heads, but for the most part, every home has a Bible in it that's read at least once a day."

Conrad rubbed his sore neck. "How long before Snow Falls becomes Los Angeles?" he wondered. "How long before the world tries to turn my twins into monsters?" Conrad turned back to the office window. "I guess I'll always worry and feel helpless...but I'll never stop fighting to protect my family, those I love...and this town."

"Including Amanda?" Andrew teased.

Conrad felt a grin touch his face. "Yeah, I guess so...even that loudmouth Brit."

Andrew began to tease Conrad a little more in order to help the guy relax but stopped when he heard Andy yell. "Smoke...basement!"

"Let's go!" Pete yelled. He jumped to his feet, yanked out his gun, and charged out of Conrad's office like a bull.

"Andrew, back door!" Conrad ordered. "Put Steve at the front door! Go!"

Andrew nodded his head and followed Conrad to an old wooden door leading down to the frozen basement. The door was standing wide open. Heavy, thick smoke was pouring out. "Steve, guard the front door. Andy, hit the back door...go!" he yelled. Andy and Steve took off running to their newly assigned locations.

"Let's move!" Pete ordered and rushed down into the basement, ignoring the heavy smoke. Conrad and Andrew took off after him. "I can barely see!" Pete called out, working his way down the steps. "Be careful!"

"Right behind you!" Conrad yelled with his gun at the ready. "There's no way he can escape this time!"

Pete reached the bottom of the stairs, squinted into the smoke, and saw a shadowy figure standing next to the table that Senator Mayfield's body had been placed on. "There!" he yelled and vanished into the smoke. Conrad chased after him. Andrew followed close behind.

"You…at the table…hands in the air!" Pete ordered. "Hands in—" Before Pete could finish his sentence, the lights went out, casting the basement into a thick, cold darkness.

Now, three smart cops would have—or at least should have—used whatever common sense they had gained during years of police work. Instead, Pete dove further into the darkness, struck a sewing dummy Andrew's wife had put in the basement, and began swinging his fist. Unfortunately, he struck Conrad right in the nose. In return, Conrad—who thought he was being attacked by either Alvin the Great or the second unknown villain— grabbed Pete and slung him toward the stairs. Pete collided into Andrew, who, in return, grabbed poor Pete by his waist and began trying to tackle the man. Pete stumbled backward into Conrad. Conrad grabbed Pete. Pete, assuming he was being attacked by two unknown intruders, began punching Andrew and Conrad in the face while both men struggled to take him down.

While Conrad, Pete, and Andrew fought with each other, Alvin grabbed Senator Mayfield's body and managed to shove it out of one of the basement windows that he had cleared snow away from and then escape himself, leaving three grown men punching and kicking each other.

"I've got him…" Conrad yelled, punching poor Pete.

"No…I've got him!" Andrew insisted and punched Pete in his gut.

Poor Pete was so out of breath that he couldn't speak, let alone let Conrad and Andrew know that they were attacking the wrong man. By the time Conrad and Andrew had him on the floor in a pair of handcuffs, he was black and blue all over.

"Hit the lights!" Conrad ordered Andrew. Andrew ran to the light switch sitting on the back wall close to the table Senator Mayfield's body had been lying on, ran back to Conrad, and looked down at the floor. The smoke, although still heavy, was beginning to thin out, allowing Conrad to clearly see that the man lying on the floor was…Pete.

"Pete?" Conrad gulped.

"Pete?" Andrew whimpered.

Pete threw a pair of red, glaring eyes up at Conrad and Andrew. "Get these handcuffs off me, you idiots," he said, using every breath he could muster to speak. Conrad winced and then quickly freed Pete. Pete rubbed his wrists and then wiped blood from his nose and lip. "One of you help me stand up."

Conrad winced again, helped Pete to his feet, and then prepared for a beating. "Now Pete…it was dark…how were we supposed to know…"

"Yeah…dark." Andrew cowered down.

Pete checked his split lip and then spit blood out of his mouth. "So. Where is the body?" he asked and then nodded his head toward the open basement window. "While you two morons were busy beating the snot out of me…oh…what's the point!" Pete threw his hands up into the air and stormed up the basement stairs.

Conrad winced, slapped a little smoke away from his face, and then looked at Andrew. "We…well…we…"

"We're stupid," Andrew told Conrad in a miserable voice.

"You said it." Conrad walked over to the basement window, climbed up on a wooden crate, looked out into the snow, and then shook his head. "The next time I ever see a magician…doesn't matter who…I'm going to shoot him!" Conrad slammed the window closed and made his way back up the basement stairs only to be met by a grinning Amanda. "Not now," he growled.

"Let the body get stolen again, huh?" Amanda asked and then made an innocent face. "Oh, did I say that? I'm sorry…not!" She laughed.

Conrad reached out his hands to strangle Amanda, but Andrew stopped him. "You shouldn't be happy about this!"

"Yes, she should be," Sarah said, appearing at the head of the hallway leading to the basement.

"I thought you were asleep," Conrad said.

"I was resting," Sarah promised. "And…waiting."

"Waiting?" Andrew asked in a confused voice.

"For Alvin the Great to show up," Sarah explained.

"You…knew?" Conrad asked and gave his wife a look that was a mixture of confusion and irritation. "Sarah, what's going on?"

"Follow me." Sarah waddled into the front room of the station and then made her way over to a fully stocked and well used coffee station. "Alvin knows we are aware of the location of the cabin he rented," she began, pouring decaffeinated coffee into a brown cup. "He seemed, at least to me, to have gone through a great deal of effort— and chance—to reclaim Senator Mayfield's body."

"That's right." Amanda nodded and pointed a hard finger at Conrad, Pete, and Andrew. "You blokes better pay attention to Detective Spencer or I'm going to smack you all senseless."

Conrad folded his arms and waited for Sarah to continue. Pete wiped at his split lip with a handkerchief and then shoved a cigar into his mouth. Andrew sighed, leaned back against the north wall of the station, and waited, still feeling stupid.

THE MORE YOU SNOW

"We seemed to have taken Alvin by surprise when we arrived at the coffee shop," Sarah continued. "Alvin was forced to leave the body of Senator Mayfield behind."

"So?" Andrew asked. "I don't follow."

"That's because you're a…dare I say…a man!" Amanda snapped, rolling her eyes at Andrew. "One of you blokes pour me a cup of coffee!" Andrew jumped and hurried to do Amanda's bidding. Amanda nodded her head at Sarah. "Go on, love."

"Well, from experience, I assumed that Alvin wouldn't venture very far from Senator Mayfield's body," Sarah continued, grinning at poor Andrew, who was terrified of Amanda. "I began thinking that Alvin might—and this was based off an assumption rather than fact—hide out in a house in town that has been vacated for the winter. After all, we did catch him hiding in the coffee shop, so it occurred to me that Alvin might not take that route again and instead seek shelter in a vacant house rather than a business."

"So my dearest and best friend began calling around to all the vacant homes we know of," Amanda eagerly cut in as she took a cup of coffee from Andrew, "and began leaving messages."

"On answering machines," Sarah clarified, taking a sip of coffee and looking at Conrad and then at Pete. "I explained in each message that the town was under lockdown due to a dangerous person being on the loose and to please remain behind locked doors instead of trying to visit the station because we had Senator Mayfield's body in the basement of the station under heavy guard."

"Now, Detective Spencer didn't know if Alvin the Great was hiding out in a vacant house or not, but she decided to throw some smoke and magic into the air herself," Amanda said in a proud voice as she smiled at Sarah. "Her plan worked."

"But you let that jerk steal the body?" Conrad asked.

Sarah sighed. "You three were supposed to capture Alvin...and not beat Pete into a glass of orange juice."

"Yeah, you clumsy blokes. You were supposed to act as a net to capture Alvin the Great." Amanda tossed an accusing eye at Conrad. "I thought you Yanks were smart. Boy, a wooden dummy is smarter than you Yanks."

Sarah fought back a grin. "The good news is that I believe I know where Alvin is hiding."

Pete took his cigar out of his mouth and gave Sarah a proud and supportive eye. "My kiddo is still a smart cop."

"Well...I may know where Alvin is hiding, but I am clueless as to where the man who assaulted you is hiding," Sarah confessed. "One step at a time, right, Pete?"

"Right." Pete nodded his head.

"Okay, it's obvious you married a dummy...so humor me and tell your husband where that body-stealing jerk is hiding."

"You're not a dummy," Sarah promised Conrad in a loving voice. "Alvin…just managed to escape again, that's all."

Conrad sighed. "The location?"

Sarah took some coffee down and then looked Conrad in his upset eyes. The poor man was desperate to prove that he was the protector and defender of the family—desperate to redeem himself in the eyes of his pregnant wife. "I believe Alvin is hiding in Mrs. Madien's home."

"Bertha's cottage?" Andrew asked.

Sarah nodded. "I called three homes," she explained. "Mrs. Madien's home is the closest home to the station…Alvin showed up in record time."

Conrad pulled out his gun. "Okay, Andrew, get Andy and Steve, we're going out into the storm."

"Hold it, you bloke," Amanda demanded and ran to a storage closet. She returned holding a fishing net. "This time, catch Alvin the Great," she pleaded. "Afterward we'll put my plan into action and try to catch the other bloke at the hospital."

Conrad stared at the net. "Pete, take the net," he said. He kissed Sarah on her cheek and rushed off to the front door of the station, determined to catch a slippery fish.

Pete shoved his cigar back into his mouth, took the net Amanda was holding, and looked at Sarah. "Good work, Detective." He smiled. "Maybe now we can make progress on this case and put some bad guys behind bars."

"Maybe," Sarah agreed. "Pete, Alvin may not be street smart…but he knows his act. If we let him escape this time, we may not find him again."

"Then let's not allow that." Pete patted Sarah on her shoulder, tossed Amanda a wink, and then nodded at Andrew. "Let's move." Andrew quickly checked his gun and then hurried after Pete, leaving Sarah and Amanda alone.

"Ten dollars those blokes beat Pete up again and let Alvin the Great escape," Amanda sighed.

"Uh…well…let's wait and see." Sarah winced and touched her tummy. Little Sarah and Little Conrad were sure moving about.

7

Conrad hunkered down behind a frozen, dark tree, keeping his head tucked down against the howling wind. "Look," he told Pete, having to speak over the deadly winds, and nodded toward the back of the gingerbread cottage sitting at the end of a sleepy street drenched with deep snow. "There's a light on in the kitchen."

Pete, who felt like a frozen penguin, studied the back of the cottage, spotted the kitchen light, and then pulled out his gun. "Andrew…Andy…cover the front of the house… Steve, take off and see if you locate a snowmobile… Conrad…you're with me," he ordered through chattering teeth that sounded loud enough to be heard clear across the world. "Andrew, give us ten minutes and then rush inside."

"Let's move," Andrew told Andy and started off into the dark storm. Steve pulled out his gun, glanced around, and vanished into the snow.

"Get the net ready, Conrad," Pete ordered. Conrad, who had been designated the "Net Man," checked the fishing net he was holding. "Ready?"

"Ready." Conrad raised his eyes up at the storm, said a prayer, and then began moving away from the frozen tree, forcing his legs to walk through knee-deep snow.

Pete carefully followed, keeping his gun at the ready. By the time they reached the back door of the cottage, both men felt as if their bodies had become icebergs. Pete was shaking so bad he doubted if his hands and eyes could cooperate enough to get off a clean shot, if needed.

"Okay…any minute now," Conrad stated, feeling his body turn from flesh to ice.

"Any…minute," Pete agreed, desperately trying to remain conscious against the storm. "Any—" he began to say again but stopped when he heard Andrew yelling orders to "get down" into the kitchen. Seconds later, a smoke bomb exploded, filling the kitchen with smoke. "Get ready," Pete ordered Conrad, pressing his face into the kitchen window and watching the kitchen fill with smoke. "He should be coming out any second!"

Conrad stepped to the side of the kitchen door and prepared the net. Seconds later, the door burst open and Alvin came thundering out on panicked legs.

"Not this time, pal!" Conrad yelled and threw the net he was holding into the icy air. The growling winds immediately caught the net and tried to yank it up into the dark night sky. However, because Conrad was standing mere inches away from Alvin, the net managed to struggle through the attack and make contact with the escaping man's body.

"Hey…what is this?" Alvin cried, feeling the fishing net fall over his body. He began throwing his panicked arms around, which caused his body to become more entangled in the net. "Hey…get me out of this thing!"

Pete stepped up to Alvin and put his gun against the man's back. "Stop moving and stand very still!" he yelled. "Conrad, cuff him!"

"Gladly!" Conrad yanked a pair of cuffs out of the left pocket of his black coat just as Andrew and Andy stepped back out into the storm. "Get the net off of this guy!"

Andrew, relieved to see that Pete's plan had worked, nudged Andy and went to work removing the net from Alvin. As soon as the net was clear, Conrad grabbed Alvin's arms, yanked them behind his back, and slapped on a pair of handcuffs. "Let's see you try to escape now, smart guy."

"Check the cottage," Pete barked at Andrew and Andy. "Find the body."

"The body…I laid the body in the snow next to my snowmobile…over there," Alvin confessed and nodded a head covered with a black ski mask toward a deep layer of woods.

Before anyone could say anything, they spotted a shadowy silhouette approaching and carrying Senator Mayfield's body. "Found it!" Steve called out.

Pete looked at Alvin. "Okay, wise guy, we're going back to the station house…and no more games, is that clear?" Alvin nodded as his mind struggled to understand how the cops had located him. "Andrew, you and Andy help Steve get the body back to the hospital and order Dr. Downing to conduct an autopsy ASAP…I don't care how busy the man is. Is that clear?"

"Pete, this storm is—" Conrad began to object, worried for Andrew, Pete, and Steve's health.

"Tough it out!" Pete barked. "We're cops, for crying out loud, not a bunch of babies!" Pete grabbed Alvin's shoulder. "Who clobbered me outside the morgue, boy? Talk! I know it wasn't you!" Pete was far too cold and cranky to play nice.

Alvin felt the bitter cold begin biting into his body. Now that he had been captured, he knew it was time to talk. "Tom Jamison."

"Mona Jamison's son?" Pete demanded. Alvin nodded. "But Tom Jamison is supposed to be in Anchorage."

"Well, the guy isn't in Anchorage, now is he?" Alvin snapped. "Look, all I want to do is take down the people who killed my old man, okay?" he barked, speaking in a normal voice, bypassing his theater tone. "My dad was murdered and Mona Jamison will do anything to stop an autopsy from being performed."

"We'll talk more at the station. Andrew, get the body to the hospital…and stay at the hospital. I'll be along when morning breaks."

Andrew drew in a weary breath. "All right, guys, let's move," he told Andy and Steve. Andy and Steve looked at each other, shrugged their frozen shoulders, and followed off after Andrew toward their snowmobiles, hoping to reach the hospital before they froze to death.

"You…move," Pete barked at Alvin.

"You heard him," Conrad told Alvin and began walking the man through the storm. An hour later, he marched Alvin into a holding cell and slammed the door closed. "Don't try to escape."

Alvin removed the black ski mask, revealing a face that appeared a little dorky…but harmless…at least to Sarah and Amanda. Alvin spotted the two women staring at him and quickly turned his face away. "I messed up."

"Why didn't you go to the police for help in the first place?" Sarah asked, relieved that Conrad and Pete had returned to the station in one piece. "We would have helped you."

"Mona Jamison would have found a way to…terminate my life, my dear detective," Alvin replied, returning to his theater voice now that two lovely women were present. "It was better for Alvin the Great to work unseen."

For some reason Sarah felt sorry for Alvin. The man was harmless and…lonely. "Conrad, get Mr. Mayfield a cup of coffee."

"Are you kidding?" Conrad asked, feeling his body slowly begin to defrost. "Sarah, this jerk is a clown!"

"No, he isn't," Sarah told Conrad in a calm voice. "It seems to me that Mr. Mayfield is a man who needs friends. Isn't that right?" she asked Alvin.

"Friends?" Alvin asked. "The only friend I ever had, my dear lady—the person who introduced me to the world of stage magic—betrayed my trust and stole the only woman I ever loved away from me. Friends? The idea is appealing...but destructive. Alvin the Great...who was once Rusty Smoke...works alone."

"And you were planning to use Senator Mayfield's murder to restart your career...alone," Sarah pointed out.

Alvin tucked his head down. "My intention, dear lady, was to capture a nest of vicious vipers with a little...shall we say...pizazz...in order to conquer justice and...yes...assist my failing career." Alvin dared to look up at Sarah and Amanda. To his disbelief, both women were staring at him the way a worried mother stares at a child who had gotten himself into trouble without realizing it. "I'm going to prison, aren't I?"

"Of course not," Sarah promised. "However, you did break into O'Mally's department store and steal some—"

"I left some cash on the shelf," Alvin cut Sarah off. "Didn't you find it?" Sarah shook her head no. "Alas, I am not a thief," Alvin sighed.

"You've been stealing a dead body, pal," Conrad pointed out.

Pete leaned back against the hallway wall opposite the holding cell and studied Alvin. The guy, in his view, wasn't all bad—misled, confused, hurt, lost, angry…a little melodramatic…but not bad. "You were trying to help, and I appreciate that. But now it's time to let the law work."

"My fellow man, if Alvin the Great hadn't paid your hospital a visit with watchful eyes, Tom Jamison would have stolen the body of one Senator Mayfield," Alvin reminded Pete. "The law, as you claim, cannot battle the head of a deadly cobra…the head, of course, being Mona Jamison."

"Alvin the Great did save the day," Amanda pointed out. "He did prevent the dead body from being stolen…by the real bad guy, I mean, not by him, of course."

Alvin tossed Pete a worried eye. "Please, let me loose. I need to get to the hospital and guard the body. Only Alvin the Great can save the day."

"Alvin the Great is staying behind bars," Conrad informed Alvin in an angry voice, which was quickly attacked by Sarah's stern eyes. "What?"

"Mr. Mayfield isn't the bad guy." Sarah reached out and took Conrad's hands. "Stop being mad at yourself, okay?"

"How can I not be?" Conrad asked. "This guy made me look like a fool in your eyes, Sarah…at a time when our twins are due to be born. So forgive me if I don't feel like being his friend." Conrad threw a hard eye at Alvin. "I want answers, understand?"

Alvin stared at Conrad for a minute or so. As he did, his mind began to understand that, yes, he had embarrassed the man in front of his pregnant wife. "Please accept my apology, Officer. I meant no harm."

"Just talk," Conrad demanded.

"My dear man, what is there to say?" Alvin asked. "Mona Jamison and her son killed Senator Mayfield."

"Proof?" Conrad asked.

Alvin lowered his eyes. "No proof…except the words of a paranoid man who is now dead…a man who confessed many secrets to me before he fled the state of Idaho out of fear for his life." Alvin let his shoulders fall. "I suppose I chased after him in a fit of…rage. You see, before Senator Mayfield fled Idaho, I overheard Mona Jamison and her son talking behind closed doors…whispering ugly little truths."

"What truths?" Conrad demanded.

Alvin slowly raised his sorrowful, angry eyes. "Senator Mayfield was going to frame me for the murder of Mona Jamison…and, of course, have me killed in the process." Alvin narrowed his eyes. "It was all a political game…the louse never cared for me…never wanted me to play on his team…never had any desire to help me become a governor. It was all a smoke act…and I walked right into it blind as a bat."

"And you heard Mona Jamison and Tom Jamison confess this?" Sarah asked.

Alvin nodded. "I needed to hear Senator Mayfield confess the same very words I heard those two…rodents… whispering. That's why I followed him to Alaska. I needed to hear the truth from his mouth." Alvin lowered his head again. "I confronted the man the night Tom Jamison left his home, but all the louse did was babble on and on about how Mona Jamison was going to have him killed. It was impossible to talk to him. When I returned the following morning…well, Senator Mayfield had vanished."

"How did you know he fled to Alaska…to Snow Falls?" Sarah asked.

"The world is complicated, but computers are not. It's not difficult, my dear lady, to track a man's personal bank card." Alvin shook his head. "Senator Mayfield was never the brightest cookie in the jar, I'm afraid. As a matter of fact, the guy was…clumsy…in his thinking. Mona Jamison, however, is not as clumsy."

"Why did Senator Mayfield choose Snow Falls?" Sarah asked Alvin, trying to keep the man on course without veering off.

Alvin shrugged. "I honestly can't answer that question, my dear lady."

Pete shoved a cigar into his mouth. "Why did Mona Jamison want the man dead?" he asked.

Alvin lifted his eyes. "Senator Mayfield, from what I managed to gather, was forming an army against Mona Jamison. He was planning to break away from her clutches and try to destroy the woman…shall we say…politically. Why? Perhaps because the louse assumed it was time to step out on his own? You see, my old man…I mean, Senator Mayfield…always did have a problem with his ego. It is my assumption that being controlled by an ugly old snake was growing tiresome to Senator Mayfield. I could be wrong."

"Senator Mayfield is dead, which means he either died of a heart attack—"

"He was poisoned," Alvin insisted, cutting Pete off. "I saw Tom Jamison leave the man's house. Tom Jamison despised Senator Mayfield. I'm positive he was sent there to poison him. There is no other possible explanation."

"But Senator Mayfield woke up in this station from a night of heavy drinking," Conrad pointed out. "Wouldn't it make more sense that the senator would have died the night Tom Jamison visited his home?"

Alvin frowned. "Yes," he confessed. "That is what troubles me. However, because Tom Jamison did try to steal Senator Mayfield's body, I am certain that he was poisoned to death…somehow. Why else would he take the risk of stealing the body?"

"I believe you," Sarah told Alvin and offered a kind smile. "Conrad, let Mr. Mayfield out of the holding cell."

"What?" Conrad exclaimed.

"Conrad, this man is guilty of only being…overdramatic and a bit reckless in his thinking. Nothing else." Sarah looked at Conrad with focused eyes. "The real criminals… and killers…are still loose."

Pete nodded in agreement. "Let him loose, Conrad."

"Yeah, let this poor guy loose and give him some coffee, you bloke," Amanda added.

"But…I…" Conrad rolled his eyes. "We nearly freeze to death catching him and I have to set him free," he fussed. Nevertheless, he set Alvin free and then raised a stern finger. "No tricks, pal…or else."

"You have my word, my good man," Alvin promised and gave Sarah a confused look. "I could be a dangerous liar."

Sarah reached out and patted Alvin's arm. "You're not," she said and waddled back to the front of the station and poured Conrad a cup of coffee. "Now all we have to do is figure out how to find and catch the real killer," she whispered as the storm continued to punish the little town of Snow Falls. "But how?"

Sarah had no clue that Tom Jamison was lying dead in a rental cabin far away. Sadly, the death of Tom Jamison wasn't going to stop Mona Jamison from attacking.

Dr. Downing used the landline phone to contact Conrad at the station. The poor old man was near to the point of collapse. Fortunately, Dr. Morrison had finally shown up at the hospital and was now lending a helping hand. Of course, Dr. Morrison was supposed to be retired, in a sense, and wasn't exactly rushing into any operating rooms…but help was help, and Dr. Downing was grateful. "Yes, this is Dr. Downing."

Conrad waved at Sarah and Pete. "It's Doc," he called out. Sarah hurried away from the window in Conrad's office and joined Pete at his desk.

"I conducted an autopsy. Now bear in mind I'm not a fully operational medical facility holding specifically designed medical labs—"

"Get on with it, Doc," Conrad pleaded.

Dr. Downing sat back in a brown sitting chair resting in the cramped doctors' lounge, took a sip of hot tea, and sighed. "The toxicology report I ran…to the best of my ability… does indicate that Senator Mayfield had some foreign toxin in his body at the time death. Don't ask me what because I don't have the proper tools in this hospital to run an exact investigation. Anchorage will have to narrow down the toxin and give it a name."

"Dare to toss an educated guess into the air, Doc?" Conrad asked.

Dr. Downing listened to the storm scream and howl outside the window in the doctors' lounge. "Senator Mayfield has an ugly liver and a failing gut, but his heart was strong…no blockages. However, the cause of death is most certainly from a massive heart attack. I would suggest that the toxin caused the heart attack." Dr. Downing grew silent for a few seconds. "Conrad," he finally spoke, "I found small traces of the toxin in Senator Mayfield's bloodstream, but the highest amounts were found in his heart. It's almost as if...something turned the heart into a magnet for the toxin? Of course, I'm beyond the point of exhaustion so my mind is simply babbling."

"Doc—"

"And it does seem that it did take a while for the toxin to break down," Dr. Downing continued. "It appeared that the toxin was beginning to harden and something caused it to start breaking up."

"Doc, make sure you record the autopsy and file your findings in a secure location. When the storm ends, you can send an electronic copy of your report to Anchorage," Conrad told Dr. Downing. "We do have an unknown assailant on the loose that may want to make sure your findings do not go public."

"Of course," Dr. Downing assured Conrad. "I'll be in touch."

Conrad put down the phone and began to explain the news to Sarah and Pete, but his office phone rang again before he could. "One second," he said, expecting a tired doctor to be calling again in order to say something that had slipped his mind. "Doc?"

"No, this is Maye Bethel out on Snow Flake Road. I'm standing at my living room window and I'm seeing a whole lot of flames coming from the woods. Only thing that's back there is a few rental cabins. You better get a firetruck out here."

Conrad glanced at Sarah. "Maye Bethel…she's reporting a fire…possibly a rental cabin," he explained. "Mrs. Bethel, we'll get a truck out as soon as we can. The roads are snowed under and—"

"The fire will be out by the time you get here…yeah, I know," Maye complained. She ended the call and continued to study the flames in the far distance.

"Sarah—"

"I know," Sarah said in a quick voice and moved behind Conrad's desk. "I'm checking."

Conrad rubbed his neck and watched Sarah check the rental cabins that were located near Maye Bethel's place. "The only cabin that's rented out that way is the Moose Cabin…rented to a T.L. Howards."

"Howards is the last name of Tom Jamison's biological dad." Sarah shot her eyes up and saw Alvin standing in the doorway of Conrad's office. "T.L. stands for Tom Lance."

Conrad continued to rub the back of his neck. "Okay…I'll call Andrew and have him round up the volunteer firefighters and get out to the cabin. In the meantime, Dr. Downing did find a toxin in Senator Mayfield's body. Looks like he may have been poisoned after all."

Amanda stepped up beside Alvin. "It's going to be daylight soon and it's been a long night…and it's probably going to be a long day. Why don't you go rest?"

Alvin looked around at four concerned faces and decided that if he was going to have any wits and strength to fight Mona Jamison, he would have to succumb to at least a few hours of sleep. "As you wish, my dear lady. But first, beware, if Tom Jamison is dead…Mona Jamison is close."

"The woman is in Anchorage," Conrad told Alvin.

"So it seems," Alvin said in a confused voice and roamed away.

Conrad let out a heavy, tired breath and called Andrew. "We have a fire at Moose Cabin. Records show T.L. Howards is staying there. Alvin said Howards is Tom Jamison's biological last name. You better round up the volunteers. I'll call the plows and see if we can get some of the snow knocked back."

Andrew fought back a yawn. He had been napping on a bed in one of the examining rooms. "Plows can't fight this snow, Conrad. It's better if we let the fire burn itself out. Besides, we're not going to pull Phil and the rest of the guys out of bed at this hour to go out into this storm."

Conrad looked at Sarah and Pete with sleepy eyes of his own. "Andrew said the plows won't be able to get through…and that Phil and the rest of the volunteers will probably resist the call."

"We'll get out to the cabin when the storm lets up," Andrew assured Conrad, yawning, and then shook his head. "I need some coffee…but in the meantime, Dr.

Downing finished his autopsy and the body is still being guarded…we haven't had any problems at this end."

"I think I know why," Conrad replied in an ominous voice.

Andrew yawned again. "I'm going to get some coffee and call my wife. Call me if anything else hits the radar."

"Will do." Conrad ended the call with a weary hand. "Looks like Moose Cabin is going to have to burn itself out."

"Looks that way," Pete agreed, tossing a cigar into his mouth and then stretching his back. "You know," he said, looking around at his dear friends, "I know this case has been a strange, rough ride, but standing here with you guys…in this snowstorm…it's not so bad."

Sarah smiled and took Pete's hand. "I'm grateful you're moving to Snow Falls, Pete. I've missed you."

"And I've missed you, kiddo." Pete smiled back. "I'm going to miss Los Angeles…well, the way the city once was…but deep down I knew the time was arriving for me to leave. I kept fighting the truth, insisting that Old Pete was going to be buried up in the canyons overlooking the city…and up until a couple of weeks ago it did seem that way." Pete examined his cigar and continued. "There comes a time when a man has to let go."

"I feel the same away about London," Amanda stated and took a sip of hot coffee. "I miss London, but the city has turned into a sour pot of corruption and misery."

"The same for New York," Conrad added. "New York isn't like it used to be in those old black-and-white movies."

"No city is," Pete clarified, walking back to the office window and looking out at the storm. "We're being pushed into little corners of the world...sad but true. But at least in this small corner, in this small town, we can hold the fort down."

Sarah watched Pete studying the storm and began to remember the life she had once lived in Los Angeles as a homicide detective. Memories of her old life...her once beautiful home...her ex-husband...the beach...the canyons...Mansion Lane...the crowded freeways...the bright sunshine and palm trees...began carrying her mind back through time. "There was a 'Once Upon a Time,'" she whispered in a sad voice as her mind walked through an empty house that had a large tree sitting in the backyard —a house that Sarah once called home. The house, once filled with the smell of coffee, flowers, and life, now stood empty, consumed with shadows and sadness, crying out for Sarah with teary eyes. "Sometimes letting go is the hardest thing to do...but..." Sarah lowered her hand and touched her tender, pregnant tummy. "Sometimes what the future holds is far better."

"Amen, love." Amanda smiled. "Sometimes—" she began but stopped when the telephone sitting on Conrad's desk rang again. "Answer the call, you bloke."

Conrad rolled his eyes and picked up the phone. "Detective Spencer, how can I—"

"This is Mona Jamison. A staff member at your hospital has informed me that an autopsy was performed on my husband. Is that true?" Mona snapped at Conrad with deadly fangs.

"Yes, an official autopsy was performed on Senator Mayfield," Conrad confirmed. "The findings indicated that there was a toxin found in his body that could have contributed to the sudden heart attack." Conrad had no idea what staff member contacted Mona Jamison, but he assumed it was probably Nurse Gwen Hallows, a snotty woman who had moved from Seattle to Snow Falls with her husband a few months back—the type of woman who hated morality and defended immorality. "The official report will be sent to the state capital—"

"You had no right!" Mona yelled. "I did not give you my permission. You were ordered to wait for the governor—"

"Mrs. Jamison…sue us," Conrad growled. "Besides, you of all people should want to know the truth…unless you're trying to hide something. If you are, we will discover the truth."

Ryan Elderson, who was hearing the entire conversation take place on speaker phone, eased over to the hotel room door, grabbed his coat, and waved a hand at Mona. "I'm not taking the fall," he called out. "You can try and kill me if you want."

"Get back—" Mona began to yell, but Ryan escaped before she could order the coward to stand down. And then, something very strange happened. Mona Jamison began to feel…panic…enter her heart. Senator Mayfield had managed to turn some of her "allies" against her, and with Ryan Elderson deserting the sinking ship, Mona wasn't sure who she had to turn to for help. Too many people wanted to destroy her, and very few wanted to see her remain in power, controlling the shots from behind the curtains. The fact was, Ryan Elderson was Mona's last chance to remain in power.

There was only one thing left to do: kill Tom Jamison and blame the death of Senator Mayfield on her son. Yes, that was the only reasonable and practical choice left to utilize. "I will be arriving in your town as soon as the storm permits," she hissed and slammed down the telephone. "Now…time to make another call." Mona hurried to her black purse and yanked out the phone number to a deadly assassin she had hired in the past to kill off certain people who were standing in the way of her political ambitions. "Hello, this is Mona."

Roger Bates put down the barrel belonging to an M-16 rifle and locked his eyes on a clear, warm beach. "What?" he asked in a hard voice.

"Snow Falls, Alaska…kill Tom Jamison…frame him for murder," Mona stated. "One million dollars when job is complete."

"Done."

Mona felt the panic gripping her heart and slowly took a deep breath. "Kill whoever stands in your way."

"Done." Roger ended the call and went back to cleaning

the barrel. "I was wondering when you were going to call me," he said with a grin, looking out at the warm beach, and then continued to clean the barrel in his hand. "I'll be leaving for Alaska very soon. And I might even pay that famed detective a visit for killing one of my heroes."

Sarah, who was unaware that Mona Jamison had hired a killer in a desperate attempt to salvage her life, walked out of Conrad's office and made her way back to the coffee station. She was hungry and wanted a donut, even though the donuts were stale. "Well," she yawned, picking out a plain donut from a brown box, "this storm has us all tied down. I think I'm going to eat my donut and go rest."

Amanda grabbed a chocolate donut before Conrad could and stuck her tongue out at him. "As you Yanks say...you snooze, you—"

"Lose. Yeah, yeah, stick it in your ear," Conrad barked at Amanda and settled for a plain donut. "Pete?"

Pete lit his cigar and shook his head no. His eyes were worried.

"Pete?" Sarah asked.

"Why would Mona Jamison travel to Alaska knowing that her husband's body has been examined?" Pete asked and then tossed a thumb out at the snow. "And if that woman is in Anchorage...why is there a cabin burning down out in the woods? Where is Tom Jamison? My gut is telling me we have trouble on the way...serious trouble."

"Oh man," Amanda fussed and kicked the floor. "Why does this always happen to us, love?" she asked Sarah. "All we wanted to do was attend the sale at O'Mally's and buy some lovely dresses. And now look at us. Trapped in a storm with trouble on the way—as if Alvin the Great wasn't enough trouble."

Conrad took a bite of his donut. "All we can do is wait," he said and nodded his head at the front door. "That storm isn't going to let anyone standing here move unless it's by skis, snowshoes, or snowmobile. But the wind is sharp enough to cut a man in half…"

"So we wait," Sarah said. She studied her donut and began to take a bite. As she did, something very scary and amazing happened: Little Sarah and Little Conrad decided it was time to enter the world outside of their mommy's tummy. Sarah let out a cry, grabbed her stomach, and looked at Conrad with wide, terrified eyes. "Uh…I…think it's time…"

"It's time!" Amanda screamed. She wet her pants and then ran out the front door of the station to go and get Dr. Downing. Poor Pete had to catch the hysterical woman before she froze to death and drag her back inside. "It's time…oh…it's time!"

So much for a calm and confident friend who was supposed to be a skilled midwife. Nope. Panic was the new fad in Snow Falls, Alaska—panic caused by two little twins anxious to meet the real world; or so it seemed.

8

Conrad helped Sarah lie down on a cot resting in one of the three holding cells. "Pete is calling the hospital. I'm sure Dr. Downing will be here soon," he said, trying to speak in a soothing voice as Sarah hugged her tummy.

"My water hasn't broken…that's good," Sarah replied, feeling contraction pains that seemed to have started in her lower abdomen instead of her upper abdomen.

"It's time…oh…it's time!" Amanda yelled and began shaking poor Alvin like he was a piñata. "It's time…the twins are coming…in the snow…"

"Aren't you a trained midwife?" Conrad barked. "Get in here!"

"I…uh…" Amanda began to reply and then…well…she simply fainted and hit the floor.

"Oh brother." Conrad rolled his eyes. "Take care of her!" he barked at Alvin.

Alvin stood frozen. He had never seen a woman go into labor before and knew no amount of stage magic was going to save the day. "I…is she really going to have a baby?"

"Two," Conrad pointed out. "Twins."

"Twins…good…lovely…a miracle…yes…" Alvin mumbled and then, like Amanda, felt his world turn dark and passed out cold.

"Oh brother!" Conrad yelled.

"It's…okay," Sarah promised, taking deep breaths. "I… think these are fake labor pains…"

"Fake labor pains?" Conrad asked, feeling as if he were ready to pass out himself.

"Contraction pain started down here…" Sarah pointed to her lower abdomen. "I read that actual labor pains start in the upper abdomen…and when I turned over to my side…" Sarah rolled over to her right side with the help of Conrad, "the pain eases some…"

"False labor—" Conrad began to say but was cut off by a panicked Pete. "What?"

"Dr. Downing can't make it…storm is too bad…wind chill is too dangerous to go out in…" Pete stated, breathing hard and sweating buckets.

"Sarah seems to think she's having false labor pains," Conrad explained.

"I…believe that's the case," Sarah said, trying to calm Pete down.

"False labor…" Pete rubbed his forehead. "Well…let's hope that's the case."

Sarah felt the pain starting to ease and smiled. "Maybe…gas?"

"Gas?" Pete asked and then started to laugh. "Kiddo…you nearly gave me a heart attack."

Conrad, out of relief more than humor, started to laugh, too. "Gas…it's either gas or fake labor pains…and look at those two!" Pete looked down at poor Amanda and Alvin the Great and burst out laughing all over again. Sarah couldn't help but to join him.

Matters were not so funny back in Anchorage. Ryan Elderson decided that running away from Mona Jamison might not have been wise. The last thing in the world he wanted to do was spend the rest of his life looking over his shoulder at every shadow. No. Besides, Mona was up in the hotel room she had rented all alone…no one was there to protect her. If Ryan managed to kill her and get away with it, not only would he be in the clear of any wrongdoing concerning Senator Mayfield, but maybe he could make a deal with Tom Jamison and have the man join his side (of course Ryan assumed Tom was still alive).

"It has to be done," Ryan whispered, riding the fancy elevator back up to the floor Mona's room was located on. "It has to be done." Ryan quickly checked an ugly gun he had hidden in the inside pocket of his coat and then stepped off the elevator.

Mona, who was unaware that she was about to die, decided to call Tom. When she received no answer, the woman hissed and wandered into the large bathroom and turned on the shower. "I'll take a hot shower and rest," she decided, struggling to calm her nerves. "I'll take—" Mona was interrupted when she heard the room door open and then close. She threw her head out of the bathroom and spotted Ryan. "Oh, it's you...you decided to come back," she spat.

Tom nodded his head and then, without saying a word, pulled the gun from his coat pocket. "Mona, it has to be this way. I can't spend the rest of my life running from you."

Mona's eyes grew wide with fear and shock. "You can't kill me...you'll mark yourself! My people will hunt you down!"

"Your people are thinning out, Mona. You're old...I'm old. The political scene is looking for fresh, young faces. That's why Raymond Alvin Mayfield has a good chance at winning the next governor's race." Ryan stepped toward Mona. "Raymond would have won the race, too, if his old man hadn't betrayed him...and it's a shame you had the man killed. Mayfield had potential...and guts."

Mona watched Ryan take another step toward her. Was she really going to die at the hands of a coward—a spineless jellyfish she controlled? "Get away from me," she hissed and threw her eyes into the bathroom. Even if she escaped into the bathroom Ryan would easily be able to wait her out. Mona's cell phone, along with the room phone, was out of reach. She was…disabled. "Get away from me!"

Ryan took another step toward Mona. "Your son will understand," he said. "Tom understands how wicked you are. After all, you tried to kill him, too."

"You…can't do this!"

"It must be done, Mona." Ryan aimed his gun at Mona. "Into the bathroom…now!" he ordered.

Mona felt her panic return in full force. The only thing that was left to do was make a mad dash toward the room phone. As she did, Ryan grabbed her arm, slung her body into the bathroom, and then slammed the bathroom door. Twenty minutes later, Mona Jamison was lying dead, fully clothed, in a hot bath holding a hair dryer. Yes, what was good for the goose was certainly good for the gander.

"See you around," Ryan told Mona. He put his gun away and slipped out of the hotel room unseen and unheard and made it safely to the Anchorage airport, where he waited for a flight back to Boise.

Roger Bates, who was preparing to leave the beach bungalow he was living in, had no idea that Mona Jamison was dead. No, the deadly killer was focused on meeting a cab, going to a small airport, taking a flight to the mainland, and then flying to Alaska and carrying out some "official" business, which included ending the life of Detective Sarah Garland, who was now Detective Sarah Spencer—and Sarah's death, of course, would come at no additional charge. But as Roger stepped out of an orange bungalow carrying a guitar case holding a dissembled sniper rifle, he was met by two men wearing gray suits. Roger immediately knew who the men were and began backing up toward the front door attached to the bungalow. "Help you?" he growled, feeling out of uniform wearing a stupid blue and red beach shirt and a pair of tan pants.

"It took us a while to locate you, Mr. Bates," one of the men said, speaking in a thick Russian voice, "but we did." The man reached into his coat pocket, pulled out a Glock 19 with a silencer attached to the barrel, and ended Roger's life before the man could turn and run. Because the bungalow Roger called home sat alone on a remote part of the beach, no eyes saw him die. "It is done," the man who shot Roger said and walked away with the second man and vanished.

And that's how Sarah's last and final murder case ended—with three deadly people each dying or being killed. Sarah never became aware that Mona Jamison had hired a killer to gun down Tom Jamison—a hired assassin who was going to gun her down as well for killing the Back Alley Killer. All that Sarah eventually found out after the snowstorm ended and Snow Falls began digging itself out was that Mona Jamison had been found dead in her hotel room in Anchorage from what appeared to be an apparent suicide.

As far as Tom Jamison was concerned, his body was found burned to a crisp in a cabin that had been set ablaze by a stove that had caught on fire. Tom Jamison's body had to be identified using his dental records. Of course, the death of Tom Jamison made Sarah, Conrad, and Pete wonder who killed the man and if the killer was still loose in Snow Falls—assuming Tom Jamison had been killed.

But at the end of two weeks, it seemed that no killer was lurking about in Snow Falls. Irony? Justice? No one ever really knew for sure. Murder had a way of attacking in waves, in the form of creepy snowmen wearing black leather jackets, haunting the dreams of a tormented woman…and then being dragged out into a deep sea and drowned.

What was certain in the life of Sarah Spencer was that the strange case of Alvin the Great had officially ended her career as a homicide detective. After the storm cleared, murder never plagued the town of Snow Falls ever again, allowing Sarah and the people she loved to settle down into a peaceful winter wind.

Poor Alvin seemed to have become a lost puppy. Murder, it appeared, had brought another stray into Sarah's life. Yes, Alvin the Great had become a lost stray that needed a home.

"Oh, I wish our twins would stop being so stubborn," Sarah sighed as she rubbed her tummy, sitting in the warm kitchen of her cabin. "I'm ten days past due…and feel like I'm going to explode."

"You look like you're going to explode," Manford told Sarah and winced. "You look like you have two bowling balls inside of your tummy."

"Don't you have to get to work?" Sarah asked Manford in a tone that told Manford it would be very wise to leave the cabin.

"Yeah…uh…Pete, drive me to work," Manford pleaded. He ran to the back door on his short legs, grabbed his coat, and hurried outside.

Pete rolled his eyes, shoved a cigar in his mouth, and looked at Sarah. The poor woman was sitting at the kitchen table wearing a…well…a plain, kinda drab, gray wool dress that wasn't very flattering, waiting for Conrad to take her to visit Dr. Downing. "Alvin, keep her company, okay? Conrad should be out of the shower in a few minutes."

"As you desire, my dear man," Alvin promised Pete.

"And speak English, man," Pete complained, rolling his eyes. He grabbed his overcoat off the back of a kitchen chair. "I have to meet our realtor for lunch, kiddo. I won't be back until later."

"You have the check, right?" Sarah asked.

"I have the check," Pete smiled and then kissed Sarah on her forehead. "My wife will be arriving in Snow Falls tomorrow…the cabin will be ours by then."

Sarah patted Pete's hand. "Drive safe, Pete."

Pete smiled and began to walk to the back door but then paused. "You know, I've been thinking," he said.

"About Tom Jamison?" Sarah asked, reading Pete's eyes.

Pete nodded. "Maybe the guy was killed and maybe he wasn't," he explained. "And maybe whoever killed him, if he was killed, went after Mona Jamison. But what is important…" Pete paused and chewed on his cigar for a few seconds. "What is important," he continued, "is that it seems that they were the target and not you." Pete pointed at Alvin. "It's been confirmed that the toxin found in Senator Mayfield's body is what caused his heart attack. The toxin was activated by alcohol that began to…I guess you can say…melt the toxin that began hardening in the guy's blood stream. I guess that's why it took longer than expected for the heart attack to occur. Who knows?"

"What's your point? I mean…respectfully, what are you implying?" Alvin asked, feeling dorky in the green and white striped sweater he had chosen to wear for the day. Yes, Alvin the Great was turning out to be a dud, just like Rusty Smoke.

Pete shrugged. "If I were you, I'd stay out of Boise, that's for sure," he continued in a serious voice. "And…well… Snow Falls isn't such a bad little town. I mean, I know there's isn't much opportunity for a magician, but I'm sure if we put our minds together, we could think of something."

"Are you saying you want me to…stay?" Alvin asked in a confused voice. "I've only been hanging around because I wanted to hear the report on Senator—I mean, my old man," he said, forcing his mouth to speak in a normal tone, skipping his usual theater voice. "That report came through last night. I…just came by to say goodbye."

"I know, I know," Pete told Alvin and tossed a thoughtful eye at Sarah. Sarah, who was feeling very grumpy, felt her heart begin to smile. Pete was up to something, and she knew what the old fart was thinking. "You said that Senator Mayfield didn't leave you a penny, right?"

"Yeah, that's what his attorney told me two days ago." Alvin sighed. "I didn't expect much, anyway."

"Son, you don't have a lot of money," Pete pointed out. "You said that yourself."

"I have a little money," Alvin replied. "I mean…I'm not dripping with dollars, if that's what you mean."

Pete winked at Sarah. Sarah smiled. "You know, Alvin," he said as he chewed on a worn-down cigar, "the cabin my kiddo is buying me and the wife today isn't a match box. There's plenty of room…and, well, I was talking to the wife last night and we agree that it would be nice to have a live-in security guard."

"A what?" Alvin asked.

"A live-in security guard…what are you, deaf?" Pete barked. "Now here's the deal. You're going to come live with me and the wife and earn your keep by using that stage magic of yours to keep the cabin safe. In return, you

get a bedroom, food, and hot water. As far as money…
well, there's work in this town…somewhere."

Alvin could barely believe his ears. "Are you…offering
me a home…after all I did?" he asked, staring into Pete's
rough but caring eyes.

"Yes, son, I'm offering you a home…and a family." Pete
walked over to Alvin, put his hand down on a confused
shoulder, and said: "It's a cold world out there, son…and
it's even colder when a person doesn't have people he can
trust and love. If you want…we would like to become
your…family. I know that's not an easy thing for you,
but—"

Alvin exploded to his legs before Pete could finish,
wrapped his arms about the old fart, and burst out into
tears that cleaned his grieving heart. "Yeah…I mean…my
dear man…I…want a family…yes…I want a family! I
want to be loved!"

Pete didn't know what to do…so he carefully hugged
Alvin back and looked down at Sarah. Sarah smiled. The
stray—Alvin the Great—now had a new home.

Yes, even in the dark alleys of murder a ray of bright
sunshine can break through.

Another week passed, and Sarah was about ready to pull
her hair out. She dreamed of going into labor each night,
praying for the moment to arrive with a desperate heart.

Dr. Downing, of course, just kept telling Sarah that her twins would arrive when they felt ready. "Well, they sure seemed ready during the snowstorm," Sarah griped at the crazy doctor before waddling out of his cabin with Amanda at her side. "And you…don't faint on me this time," she fussed, stepping out into a clear day holding a bright, icy blue sky beaming down on a white wonderland.

"Boy, are you cranky, love." Amanda winced and then dared to look at the ugly pink, red, purple, and yellow coat Sarah had bought at O'Mally's the day before. The coat was…atrocious. Of course, Amanda didn't say a word. The last thing Amanda wanted to do was get slugged by her dearest, closest, best friend in the world. Besides, she was wearing a really stylish brown and white coat that made her appear very British—why upset a pregnant woman over a bad fashion choice?

"Oh…drive me home," Sarah fussed, allowing Amanda to help her navigate an icy driveway. "All I want to do is lie down and rest."

Amanda winced and helped Sarah into the passenger seat of her truck. "Homeward bound," she promised and carefully drove Sarah back to her cabin.

Now, what happened next showed how the mighty hand of Love, a Hand that came from gracious God, showed Sarah just how much she was loved and how people like Alvin the Great, although odd and strange, were in fact sent to play a vital role in her life.

Alvin was shoveling rock salt onto Sarah's driveway when Amanda appeared. He waved and moved over to the side of the yard in order to allow room for Amanda's truck. Sarah sighed. Alvin was always at her cabin doing nice things. It was as if the poor guy felt the need to earn people's affection. What Sarah didn't know was that Alvin started having dreams that Sarah was going to go into labor any day and wanted to stay close. Why? Because in the dreams he was the one who was assigned to deliver her twins. Yes, a dorky magician who had somehow survived a strange murder case, one that left everyone a bit uneasy and uncertain, knew he was on a mission to make sure the twins entered the world safe and sound.

"It's going to snow tonight," he explained, hurrying over to Amanda's truck and helping Sarah get out. "Rock salt never hurts."

"Oh…well…thank you," Sarah sighed. She patted Alvin on his arm and began to waddle toward the kitchen door.

"I have to drive into town to get some groceries, love. I'll check on you when I get back," Amanda called out.

"I'll keep an eye out," Alvin promised.

"She's mighty grumpy," Amanda warned.

"I heard that, June Bug!" Sarah yelled. "I hope you get four flat tires and get stuck in a snowbank!"

"See?" Amanda winced, climbed back into her truck, and drove away like a woman escaping the mouth of a cruel drill sergeant, leaving poor Alvin behind enemy lines.

Alvin watched Sarah waddle into the cabin and finished laying down the rock salt. After putting the salt away, he stood out in the icy cold for a few minutes, soaking in the natural beauty of the snow and cold, seeing himself as a rugged lumberjack—even though he was wearing a nerdy yellow coat that made him look like a bottle of mustard—and then ventured into Sarah's cabin. "It's a pretty day out there," he said in a cheerful voice.

Sarah nodded her head as she worked to sit down at the kitchen table holding a turkey sandwich and a cup of coffee. "Yes, I suppose it is, Alvin," she said. "I suppose —" Sarah suddenly stopped talking and grew very silent.

"What?" Alvin asked in an alarmed voice, watching Sarah's eyes grow wide and white.

"I…think…my twins are going to be ready to wear their first diaper…" Sarah whispered and quickly pointed at the kitchen telephone. "Alvin …call Dr. Downing…and then call Conrad…"

Alvin watched Sarah put down her sandwich and coffee and grab her tummy. Panic entered his heart—well, panic tried to enter Alvin's heart. But then he felt the presence of a loving angel appear over him. A sudden calm washed over him as if a soothing wave of absolute peace had crashed down onto the shores of his heart.

"Okay, just stay calm…and…I promise not to faint this time." Alvin rushed over to the kitchen telephone and tried to call Dr. Downing's phone, reading the phone number off a piece of paper taped next to the phone. "Uh…Sarah, there's no dial tone?"

"Oh…that's right, the phone lines are being worked on." Sarah pointed to her purse. "My cell…phone…hurry."

Alvin ran to Sarah's purse and fished out her cell phone. "Uh…your phone is saying there's no service?"

Sarah let out a loud cry. "Alvin…my twins are coming… these are not fake labor pains…help me into the living room…please." Alvin grabbed Sarah's arm and helped the precious woman walk into the living room and sat her down on the couch. As he did, Amanda walked through the back door. "Amanda…in here…"

"I came back to apologize, love," Amanda called out, stomping snow off her boots. "I know you're—"

"In labor!" Alvin yelled.

"In labor," Amanda continued. "I understand that being pregnant with twins is…" Amanda stopped talking and let Alvin's words sink in. "In labor?" she cried out and dashed into the living room where she saw Sarah lying on the couch. "I…stay calm…I'll call—"

"Phone is down…cell phone doesn't have any service…" Sarah said, breathing hard, and then let out a loud cry. "Oh…the twins are coming…"

Amanda…well…she wet herself again and then fainted all over again, leaving Alvin all alone. Alvin didn't know what to do. All of his life, deep down, he wanted to be a hero instead of a lonely dork; a man people respected instead of tossed pennies at to do a few silly vanishing acts. Boy, had he made a fool of himself trying to restart his career while "defending justice" by stealing a dead body and causing Sarah a headache.

But now, as he looked down at Sarah—a beautiful woman who had become like a sister to him—Alvin knew that the time to finally be a hero had arrived. "I can do this," he whispered. He bent down, patted Sarah's shaky hands, and offered a soothing smile. "I've been reading on how to deliver babies…looks like Alvin the Great is going to become Dr. Mayfield today…just stay calm…I need hot water and some sheets."

"You…no …get me to the truck…drive me to the hospital," Sarah begged and then let out another loud cry. "Oh…no time…twins…on their way…now…"

Alvin dashed away for a few minutes, finally returning with a large plastic green tub full of hot water and an armload of ripped bed sheets. "Okay, Sarah…here we go…just promise me that I can teach the twins a little stage magic when they get older…and maybe…the twins can call me Uncle Alvin?"

"You…bet," Sarah promised Alvin, feeling a strange calm fill the living room. "Okay, Alvin the Great, the stage is all yours."

Alvin drew in a deep, steady breath, smiled down at Sarah with eyes that were learning what being loved by a real family truly felt like, and went to work. Sarah closed her eyes, prayed, and then did everything Alvin began telling her to do, finding it ironic that a lonely, dorky magician was delivering her twins instead of a certified doctor. Life sure was strange, she thought, glancing down at Amanda's unconscious body. Sarah would have never thought… say…ten years back…that she would be living in a small town in Alaska having a dorky magician delivering a set of beautiful twins. No, ten years ago she was an active homicide detective married to a different man, living on a quiet street in a lovely two-story home, working long hours with Pete and chasing down deadly killers. The thought of living—or even visiting—Alaska had never crossed Sarah's mind. No, her life was consumed with crowded freeways, palm trees, dry canyons, fancy mansions, bright sunshine, warm beaches…corruption and murder; a life that Sarah clung to with desperate hands.

But then her life had been snatched away…shattered by divorce…and Sarah had found herself living in a small town in Alaska, where she met a strange, funny British woman who became a sister to her. However, a dark, deadly snowman followed Sarah to Alaska, chasing her into one murder case after the next, desperately trying to destroy her life. In the end, Sarah had managed to kill the snowman, remarry, and begin a new life that she adored in the small Alaska town, eventually becoming pregnant with her twins. And now…she was lying on a brown couch having a dorky—but caring—magician who needed a family and love delivering her twins.

"One…thing…before my twins arrive?"

"Yes?" Alvin asked.

"How did you escape the coffee shop?" Sarah asked and then…whoa momma…did the pain get real.

"Alvin the Great must never reveal his secrets." Alvin smiled, patted Sarah's foot, and went to work becoming "Dr. Mayfield." What neither Sarah nor Alvin knew was that if Alvin had not decided to come over and shovel rock salt onto a snow-soaked driveway that morning, Sarah would have been thrust into danger and forced to deliver her twins alone because poor Amanda would have passed out regardless. Yes, in the end, the story always had a strange and beautiful way of bringing in the oddest characters to be a hero—and Alvin was certainly a hero on that cold, clear Alaska day.

"Sarah?" Alvin whispered.

Sarah, feeling as if she were going to faint, found the strength to open her eyes. She spotted Alvin holding a beautiful baby boy and a beautiful baby girl wrapped in two clean, warm blue blankets. "My…twins…" Sarah reached up her exhausted arms. Alvin carefully placed Little Conrad and Little Sarah into Sarah's arms and stood back. "My…babies…" Tears of joy began falling from Sarah's eyes as she looked into the sweetest, most beautiful faces she had ever seen. "Oh…Mommy has you…Mommy has you."

And with those words, Sarah's past life completely vanished from her mind and heart. Yes, Detective Sarah Garland officially vanished that day, leaving behind Sarah

Spencer, a new and complete woman who was now the mother of two beautiful twin babies. Sarah began a new life that day—a life filled with a peace and joy that she had, unknowingly, earned through the years.

Amanda let out a moan as her eyes fluttered open. Alvin smiled, bent down, and helped Amanda sit up. "The twins have arrived," he said in a voice that no longer sounded dorky. Yes, Alvin no longer needed to use theatrics to accompany his speech. Why? Because while delivering Little Conrad and Little Sarah, Alvin the Great died, leaving behind a person who decided it was time to face life as a new man. Yes, on that cold Alaska day…four new lives were born.

"Twins…here?" Amanda immediately woke up, jumped to her knees, and crawled over to the couch. When her eyes spotted Sarah holding two beautiful babies, she burst into tears. "Oh love…the twins…they're so beautiful…"

Alvin smiled, walked into the kitchen, and tried the kitchen phone again. This time, ironically, the phone was working. Alvin quickly called Conrad. Conrad about wet his pants, burst out of his office, tripping all over himself, and raced home. Pete followed.

"Sarah!" Conrad yelled, thundering through the back door, falling and crashing all over the place, and finally making it into the living room.

"I'm here…we're here," Sarah called out in a calm voice, holding Little Conrad and Little Sarah in her arms. "Come say hello to your son and daughter."

Conrad dropped down onto his knees in front of the couch and stared at his twins. The babies were both asleep in their mommy's loving arms. "They're—"

"Beautiful," Pete finished for Conrad.

Sarah looked up and saw Pete standing at the foot of the couch wiping a tear from his eye. "Pete…you made it," she said in a weak, tired, but happy voice.

"Where else would I be?" Pete smiled. "When I saw Conrad tear out of the station…Old Pete knew."

Conrad stared at his son and daughter and then reached out a shaky hand and touched Sarah's soft forehead. "You did good…"

"I called Dr. Downing," Alvin said. "He's on his way. I guess…I better be going."

"No," Sarah begged and calmly told Conrad and Pete how Alvin had delivered her twins.

"You…not…Amanda?" Conrad asked in a shocked voice, staring at Alvin.

"Well, I'll be a monkey's butt," Pete said, also in shock.

Alvin wanted to blush, and everything inside of his heart begged him to respond in a silly theater voice. Instead, he simply looked into Sarah's supportive eyes and then nodded his head. "Yes, well, when I—"

Before Alvin could finish his sentence, Manford came crashing through the back door, falling all over himself, and ran into the living room on his short little legs. "I heard…Alvin called the store…is it true?"

"It's true." Sarah smiled.

Manford moved up to the couch, spotted Sarah holding two sleeping babies, and smiled from ear to ear as an indescribable joy entered his heart—a joy that felt… well…complete. "Thanks for calling me, Alvin," he whispered. "You're a real friend."

Sarah looked up at all the faces staring down at her. She looked into the face of her husband, her best friend, her dear old friend from Los Angeles, her little man, and the strange magician, and smiled. The living room was full of people who had once been broken but now were complete and whole as one family—as one heartbeat. "I love you all," she whispered as tears of joy began falling from her beautiful eyes.

"And we love you, love," Amanda promised. She glanced at Conrad and punched his arm. "Congratulations, you bloke…I mean…dad."

Conrad smiled, bent down, and kissed his twins. "Now life truly begins," he whispered into Sarah's ear.

Sarah closed her eyes and drifted off into the most peaceful dream she had ever had…a dream filled with soft falling snow and the laughter of family. The dream wasn't filled with a hideous snowman wearing a leather jacket and chewing a candy cane. No, the snowman was dead and Sarah Spencer no longer needed to fear the unknown of her dreams because the sweetest dream of her life had become a reality.

"Let's go into the kitchen and leave them alone," Amanda whispered and, surprisingly, took Manford's hand instead of kicking the little guy.

Pete threw his arm around Alvin and together they walked into the kitchen and each had a warm cup of coffee…as a family. However, five minutes later, Conrad heard Manford let out a loud yell of pain and Amanda holler: "Thanks for drinking the last of the coffee, you little bloke!" Conrad rolled his eyes, kissed his twins, and whispered: "You'll get used to Aunt Amanda. Just be careful, she has a mean kick." Little Conrad and Little Sarah both agreed as they lay safely in their mother's arms. Sarah, who was far away in a beautiful dream…smiled.

ABOUT WENDY

Wendy Meadows is a USA Today bestselling author whose stories showcase witty women sleuths. To date, she has published dozens of books, which include her popular Sweetfern Harbor series, Sweet Peach Bakery series, and Alaska Cozy series, to name a few. She lives in the "Granite State" with her husband, two sons, two mini pig and a lovable Labradoodle.

If you enjoyed this book, please take a few minutes to leave a review. Authors truly appreciate this, and it helps other readers decide if the book might be for them. Thank you!

Get in touch with Wendy
www.wendymeadows.com

Made in United States
North Haven, CT
06 February 2024

48391755R00100